THE PEOPLE'S CANDIDATE

THE PEOPLE'S CANDIDATE

LUIS ZAENSI

ReadersMagnet, LLC

CONTENTS

CHAPTER ONE

The inspection.

It was a hot summer morning and Miami's characteristic humidity made it hotter. The small mechanical shop opens its doors at 7:00 AM and its three employees are working in their respective jobs. Nicholas Field was the owner of the workshop. Nick was forty-four years old, medium height, glasses, red hair and a beard. His Hispanic friends nicknamed him Red-Beard, and his Anglo friends nicknamed him ZZ Top.

Roberto was the second in command at the shop. He was sixty years old, tall, skinny, and totally bald. Despite his English language limitations, he was the second in command at the shop. He served as the translator who attracted many Latin clients. His erroneous translations caused many problems and confusion at the shop, but Nick valued his honesty and professionalism.

Mark was the youngest of the three. He was thirty-five years old, medium height, with brown hair and several tattoos on both arms. Mark was an expert in air conditioning. Mark was always talking about politics and never agreed with anything or anyone. He was passionate when he spoke and did not realize that Nick and Roberto paid no attention to him.

Nick had his shop in an area called Little Havana. Only with wonderful service and Roberto's help he could survive through the years. It's 9:00 AM, when a city inspector shows up at the small office.

"Good morning, Nick."

Nick felt as if instead of a greeting he had received a cold bucket of water poured on his back. They inspected him and fined him ten days ago.

"Good morning. I can see that you like my workshop. I thought it would take a little longer for you to come back."

The inspector laughs and replies. "You don't have to kill the messenger if you don't like the message."

"I think the messenger enjoys the message." Nick replies wryly.

Nick's words provoked the Cuban inspector to check if the previous violation had been corrected and to give an exhaustive review of the premises. The inspector was of Cuban origin and on the previous inspection, Roberto was the one that talked to him. The inspector passed by Roberto's side and didn't even greet him, he just said to him.

"Why aren't you wearing gloves? You were using it last time."

Roberto enraged replies. "I don't use them today because of a sexual, religious problem."

The confused inspector asks. "What does it mean? I don't get it."

Roberto had a reputation for having a rather explosive character and replies in Spanish

"I meant that because of my santos cojones."

The inspector flushed, and in his gaze, there was fire. Nick hadn't understood a word, but he had followed the conversation like watching a tennis match moving his head from side to side. That was enough to realize that things were going from bad to worse. Nick intervenes and says.

"I don't know what's going on between you two, but whatever it is you ask me, I'm the one who gives the answers."

The offended inspector replies. "I just asked him why he didn't have gloves on, and he replied with a lack of respect."

"But what did he tell you?"

The inspector shrugs and responds. "I don't know how to translate it."

Nick asks Roberto. "What did you say?"

"I don't know how to translate it either."

Nick moves his head and responds. "So that's a problem among you Cubans."

The furious inspector looks up and sees that the large exhaust fan is not working. "Why don't you have the exhaust fan working? That violates the required ventilation of the premises."

Nick closes his eyes; his frustration is visible; Nick knew the fan motor had burned out and he couldn't get it going. Nick tries to calm the mood to avoid more problems.

"You are right, the extractor motor burned out and we ordered it. I can show you the receipt for the order and the payment. Not that we are not using it. Those things happen and are out of our hands."

The inspector calms down a bit. Deep down, he feels sympathy for Nick, who is struggling to stay afloat in difficult times.

"I understand and believe me, I'm not happy to fine hard-working people like you."

Mark had stayed away but was attentive to what was happening. Tempers were calming down and Nick felt he had extinguished the fuse that had almost exploded the dynamite. Nick didn't count on Mark not only lighting the fuse again, but making sure it exploded this time.

"You are just a bunch of liberals, communist; you are all parasites who only know how to live off the work of others. You should be ashamed to come here where they are working hard to pay your salary."

Mark points his finger at him and angrily tells him. "You take the bread from the one who puts the bread on your table."

The inspector does not know from where Mark came from or who Mark was. He thinks Mark is a customer who has gotten into the conversation and responds to him.

"The conversation is with the owner of the shop and not with the customers. You should not be here in this area, that is not allowed by the insurance."

Nick feels relief that he can still fix the situation if he makes him believe Mark is a customer and before he can say a word, Mark responds.

"I'm not a client. This is where I work. I am not like you; I do work for a living."

The inspector looks at him up and down and says. "If you work here, you must wear steel-toed boots, that's the law. That's another violation."

Mark responds. "You are lucky that I'm not wearing the steel-toed boots, so when I kick your ass, it will hurt you less."

The inspector throws his notebook on the floor and screams. "Bring it on if you are so macho. I am going to kick your ass so hard that I am going to hurt your entire family."

Nick and Roberto get into the middle to avoid the fight, and Nick sends Mark to the office. The inspector picks up his notebook from the floor and writes three citations and gives them to Nick.

"This is my job, but I know no one appreciates it. I only came to check that you had taken care of the last warning and with only that, I was going on my way. You don't like my job, but that's the law, and if you don't like it, change it. I'll just enforce it."

The inspector leaves, leaving Nick with all three tickets in his hand. Nick looks at the amount of the fine and puts his hand on his forehead. He can't afford to fire Mark or Roberto from work, but he also couldn't allow to repeat an incident like this. If one thing is certain, it's that the inspector will be back in two weeks. Nick meets with Mark and Roberto in the office.

"We cannot repeat a situation like this. We cannot fight battles we know we cannot win. Roberto, I don't know what you said to him, but I know it didn't help at all and you, Mark, just sank us."

Roberto responds. "That boy came today differently; I don't know what was wrong with him. He always calls me grandpa, and he's kind, but he treated me like if I was a piece of shit, and I will not allow any brat to treat me like that."

Nick understood that he himself had unleashed the chain of problems with his unnecessary comment on the message and the messenger. Nick gets up and says. "This is a lesson for us to learn to respect the work of others, no matter how much we don't like it, and learn to control our emotions. Now let's get to work that we have already lost two hours and there are fines to pay."

Nick grabs some brake shoes he has to put on a car and the three of them prepare to leave the office when they see that the fire department inspector was parking. The three of them look at each other without crossing a word.

"Good morning, Nick. How are you doing?"

Nick drawing strength from where he no longer had responded kindly.

"Very good, thank you. How are you doing?"

"Okay, I have a job and I'm not sick. What more could you ask for? It will only be a few minutes. I must check the alarms and the extinguishers." The inspector responds with a big smile.

Nick tells him. "You know the way. Feel right at home."

Nick starts to work on the car's brakes when he hears the inspector calling him.

"Nick, can you come here, please?"

Nick takes a deep breath, closes his eyes, and tries to control himself. Roberto and Mark look at each other curiously. Nick walks slowly towards the inspector.

"What's going on Garry?"

"Your three extinguishers are empty. Look at the gages, the needles are in the red."

Nick puts his hand on his forehead and moves his head from side to side, trying to restrain himself.

"Garry, you know that I have never had problems with you. The company that I pay is supposed to check the fire extinguishers. I don't know what has happened."

"I understand you Nick, but the responsibility is yours, not the company's."

Those words were the drop that overflowed the cup. Nick threw the tool he was holding in his right hand against the wall.

"Then give me the fucking ticket, just one more for my collection. You are all the same thieves in uniforms.

Give me the fucking ticket and get that fuck out of my business."

The inspector was speechless. He never expected such a response from Nick.

"What happens to you, Nick? Why do you treat me this way? I have never disrespected you and I know that is not you. But I don't have to put up with such disrespect from you or anyone. I just wanted to warn you, but your attitude merits the tickets."

The inspector writes a ticket for each extinguisher, gives it to him, and leaves without saying a word. Nick kicks the tire of a car repeatedly while screaming at the top of his chest to vent his helplessness. Nick stops to hear Mark and Roberto's laughter. What the fuck is so funny to you?

"You told us we had to learn to control our emotions, but somehow is not working." Mark replies.

"Fuck you all, get to work, that apparently this month there will be no salary for anyone."

At the end of the day's work, Nick is sitting in his office with his arms crossed and his gaze lost. Mark watches him for a while and says.

"Don't think about it anymore. Come with me tonight and have a blast seeing me telling these ass holes what I think about them."

Nick reacts. "What are you talking about?

"Today at 8:00 PM there is a meeting at the town hall where George Martin comes to pronounce his presidential candidacy."

Nick, more confused, asks. "Who is George? What are you talking about?"

"Florida is a key state for elections, because sometimes it votes Republican and sometimes Democratic, so the brazen want to campaign here early. And he brings the ass kisser, Commissioner Martinez, to bring him the Hispanic votes and the other ass kisser, Tony Burke, to bring him the Anglo vote. I want you to see how I'm going to enjoy myself by calling him a liar. I'm going to show you I not just talking about politics, but I'm more prepared than any of them."

Nick laughs. "You're more fucked up in the head than I thought. Why don't you run if you are so good at politics?"

"Because it takes money or selling your principles and I don't have money, neither do I sell my principles."

Nick remains thoughtful and responds. "If you pick me up, I will go with you. I would love to see you make a fuss about the anthill, and at least I will have the satisfaction of seeing them defensively."

"Of course, I will pick you up. Tonight will be unforgettable. It will make you change the way you see things. "

Mark excitedly addresses Roberto. "Grandpa, do you want me to pick you up too?"

Roberto looks at him and answers. "I don't know what the fuck you're eating or smoking, but if you plan to change the world, you're really fucked up. People write and pronounce corruption and politics differently, but they have the same meaning. I don't waste my time or swim against the current."

Nick replies. "Roberto, every day we have to listen to Mark's bullshit. We will see how well he has the spurs on. At least we will have fun for a while. After a day like today, we deserve it."

Roberto surprised answers. "I can't believe you found Mark's story believable."

"No, seriously, come with us."

Roberto, trying to kill two birds with one stone, responds. "Only if Mark agrees not to talk to me about politics anymore."

Roberto was sure that Mark would not accept, but Mark answers.

"You got a deal, Grandpa. I am not just words. I will sweep the floor with them."

CHAPTER TWO

Meeting with George Martin.

In a luxurious apartment on Fisher Island, one of the candidates for the presidency from the Democratic Party named George Martin, who was a senator from the state of Pennsylvania, was meeting local politicians. These politicians, like birds of prey, tried to ingratiate themselves with him as a future political investment.

Miami Dade County Commissioner Angel Martinez is the meeting organizer. Martinez expected the best slice of the pie if George became president. Martinez addresses the group.

"Today, we have the White House, but not the Senate. That's a common thing, voters divide powers. Florida is a key state, and we have a Republican governor, which complicates the scenario for us. That doesn't mean that we can win the state. I am confident that with his leadership in the White House and the influence of the president, we can easily control this state and have a Democratic governor. I have served in the Florida Senate, was the mayor of Miami and I am currently the county committee coordinator. Under state law, I have had to leave office after the second term, but I have never been defeated at the polls. I count on the political trajectory and the support of ninety percent of the Hispanic vote, sixty percent of the Anglo support, and seventy-five percent of the black vote. If we join forces, I can be his right hand as governor of Florida."

George raises his eyebrows in amazement. "I couldn't imagine such a trajectory. If you win the governorship of Florida, you have a guaranteed a seat in the Senate, you can count on it. Just don't say the black vote, that is not politically correct. You must say the African American vote. We can't give the enemy a chance to attack us."

The group laughs and responds. "I assure you, I won't make that mistake again. Now, moving on to another topic, these are the two most important points to deal with:"

"First, inflation and the cost of housing. "

"Second, you must touch Cuba, Venezuela, and Nicaragua."

Remember that most of the Hispanic voters originate from those countries. Using "VIVA CUBA LIBRE" has become too common, so it sounds more like a mockery than a phrase of support.

George laughs again. "I thank you for letting me know. I had learned that phrase and I was going to use it today. I promise not to make that mistake. That's why I need people like you to guide me. This is teamwork, where we are all needed here."

One state north of Florida, in the city of Atlanta, Georgia, Republican Senator Barry Johnson met with politicians with the same attitude, but this time from the Republican Party. Barry asks his advisor.

"How are we in the polls?"

"We are even. The opponent who offers the greatest threat is Senator George Martin. He has a slight advantage because he today campaigns in Florida. Today he has a town hall meeting at Miami City Hall, but we already have a person who will attend the meeting and record it for us to study it and plan the counterattack."

Barry remains thoughtful and then responds. "I need you to prepare a meeting in the same place that George does his to abolish his advance. The battle will be tough, and we cannot forget that although the White House does not have much sympathy, it still maintains a significant influence on the voters."

It was 7:20 PM and in the city hall of Miami, a long line of people formed to enter the meeting with George Martin. Nick, Mark, and Roberto were in the middle of the line. When they got to the entrance, the security guard asked for the admission tickets. Nick was the first, so he turns around and asks Mark.

"Give me the admission tickets, please."

"I don't have any tickets; the radio announcement doesn't specify that you need a ticket to get in. This is a public event, not partisan or for the privileged one."

The security officer apologized and explained that seating was limited and without tickets, there was no entrance.

Mark enraged screams. "Doesn't surprise me that this brazen man really wanted to listen to the people, so he only lets in those who could not ask him what that does not suit him."

The security officer to avoid a scandal responds. "I don't give a fuck who is running or who wins the election, but you better calm down and leave on your own, or I call the police to kick you out."

Mark and Roberto turn around to leave when Nick stops them.

"Wait a moment, officer, you may not know, but the town hall is a public place that belongs to taxpayers. Holding a private event in a public venue without a permit from the city is totally illegal. They must compensate the city for such an event, so that it does not come out of the taxpayers' money. You must add to that, the false advertisement broadcast on the radio saying that it is a public event, when in fact it is for a previously chosen audience. I think you better reconsider your decision and find a space for us because this may have started here, but I assure you that this is not where it ends."

The officer was stunned by Nick's response. He did not know what to answer, so seeing that Nick, Mark, and Roberto were not leaving, he ignores them and ask the next in line for tickets. No one knew that a Haitian man named Eugene Batiste was the spy for Republican candidate Barry Johnson and was recording the incident with his cell phone. The next in line was a group of fifteen students from the University of Miami Law School who emotionally applauded Nick's response and then refused to enter if Nick, Mark, and Roberto could not enter. The security officer tried to ignore the students and calls to the next ones, but the students shouted they will block the entrance and that they will let no one pass.

Sergeant Stanley from the Miami police, hearing the uproar, immediately goes to investigate.

"What happened? What's the matter?

The security officer points his finger at Nick and responds. "This Viking and his friends want to force their way into the event, and they don't have tickets to the event."

The students scream. "That's a lie. The Viking is right. They promoted this event as public, when in fact it is private."

The sergeant, accustomed to imposing his authority, tells them to silence and then addresses Nick.

"Do you have an entrance ticket?"

"No, sergeant, I don't have one."

The sergeant believes he solved the problem with an arrogant attitude and with a superiority complex responds.

"If, as you say, the event is private and you don't have an entrance ticket, that makes it a non-criminal, civil issue. I will arrest you if you force your entrance. If you cause public disorder, I will also arrest you, and if you obstruct entry to the event, I will also arrest you. Your best option is to leave and sue the promoters of the event for false advertisement."

Senator George and Commissioner Martinez are touching on the last points of the event.

"Senator, I have given all participants a piece of paper to write a question. After you answer the questions of local journalists, a child will bring you a basket with the questions. You take out a question and put it on the podium, then read the question that is written on the sheet of your notes. Remember to look at the audience and wait for someone to stand up. We have seven people in the public already prepared for this, so we will avoid any compromising questions."

Martinez and George are interrupted by one of the event's organizers.

"Commissioner, we have problems outside. I think you should go out there to solve it. It is getting out of control."

Martinez angrily replies. "What is it so serious that you can't figure it out? If I have to solve my problems and yours, then go looking for someone else to sponsor you."

"Not commissioned. This goes a little beyond the normal. We have a Republican infiltrator in the line that wants to sabotage the event."

Martinez controlled himself so as not to slap the young man. "How can you be so stupid to give tickets to people without researching them in advance?"

"No, commissioner they don't have tickets."

Martinez loses control and yells at him.

"Then they can't come in idiot, for that you have a security officer and a police sergeant, or you need me to send you the national guard."

"It is not as easy as you think. The Viking is very well prepared. Someone trained him well before coming. He even won the support of the fifteen students from the university that you recommended and now the students are blocking the entrance. I immediately notified the sergeant and came to warn you."

George looks at Martinez and says. "You told me everything was under control. I can't start with a scandal that scares away donations. Go out right now and take care of it."

Martinez rushes out and sees the sergeant in front of Nick, surrounded by the students. Sergeant Stanley pointing his finger at Nick says.

"I will not repeat myself. You leave, or I arrest you."

Martinez felt a great relief. He thought that would be the end, but Nick responds.

"I can see that your hands don't shake to enforce the law."

Nick's words were like a command to shut up. Everyone was waiting for the response of the sergeant, who responds firmly.

"They have not shaken; they don't shake, and they will not shake. I can show it to you right now if you wish."

"Very well sergeant, finally someone has his pants on and is not afraid to face the influential. Please cancel this event immediately."

The sergeant laughs mockingly and responds. "I don't know what dog food you're eating, what are you smoking, or what the fuck you have in your head, son."

"You are wrong sergeant, as you say, this is a private event, so you can't have it in the city hall without the previous authorization from the city. The promoter must pay for the rent of the location, including your salary and that of the security officer. We taxpayers don't have to pay for politicians' expenses."

His prolonged silence showed that the sergeant was against the wall and that his famous pants had become a swimming suit. Martinez, seeing that the sergeant was not responding, comes to his aid.

"Good evening gentlemen, welcome. How can I help you?"

Before anyone can say a word, one student named Brandon says. "This is simple commissioner. Please answer. Is this a public or private event?"

The commissioner to prevent Nick's entrance and have the support of the sergeant responds sharply.

"It's a private event where we've invited the public. Maybe this has caused confusion and I understand it, but sometimes you try so hard to do things right you make mistakes."

Nick asks Martinez. "So, you followed the protocol to get the permission for the event?"

Martinez becomes offended and responds. "This is a serious event of respectable people, where the future president of the nation will be present. Not only is your comment offensive, but it obviously follows a political agenda aimed at tainting Senator George Martin's campaign."

Nick retorts. "That doesn't answer my question. Do you have the city's permission, yes or no?"

Martinez screams. "Of course. Are you satisfied or need something else?"

"Not just that, but I want to let you know that the cameras of these reporters and all these witnesses recorded you making that claim. It will be difficult for you to deny it when tomorrow morning my lawyers come with a court order to look for those city permits. Also, remember that you lied to Sergeant Stanley, and that is a crime, too. According to the sergeant, his hands do not tremble at anything or anyone."

Martinez paled; he felt a chill that almost fainted. "Wait a minute, don't take me literally. I'm not the organizer of this event. If I made that claim, it is because I find it unacceptable and highly unusual that such a failure could occur. And I came to solve the problem, not to create a problem. The reason that we give entrance tickets is not to select the audience. We must comply with the fire department regulations that limit us to a certain number of audiences according to the space of the room. But you will be my front-row guests."

Martinez goes to his assistant and unloads all his fury on him.

"Go in and bring two more of your group and you all will stay outside. Do not dare to enter until the last guest has left."

The nervous young man asks him. "Who do I take out, commissioner?"

"I don't give a fuck, you idiot. We are already fifteen minutes late."

The students laughed out loud as Martinez and his assistant practically ran away. The sergeant, who was also laughing, shakes Nick's hand and says.

"You have earned all my respect. You need balls to do something like that. You should be the one running."

The students take Nick by surprise and put him on their shoulders while shouting "THE VIKING, THE VIKING." Inside the room George was standing at the podium studying the answers he had to give to the supposed public questions that had been chosen at random. The delay and uncertainty of what was happening made him feel uncomfortable. Martinez enters the room and heads to the front row and removes three guests from their seats and moves them. George calls him and tells him. "You can't do that; those are my most valuable donors."

Martinez responds in a low voice. "It's that we have a minor problem."

"I don't give a damn about your problem; they have to be in the front row."

Martinez brings donors back to the front row and evacuates the next three seats next to the donors. Martinez is apologizing to the donors, when the security guard opens the door and the students come in carrying Nick and shouting "THE VIKING, THE VIKING." Brandon looks at Martinez who is in front of the room in front of three empty chairs and takes Nick to him and tells him. "Here's your guest of honor, as you say."

A stranger had the perfect view of the show because of Martinez giving him a front-row seat. Everything was going wrong, and he could not blame his assistant. George changed colors like a disco lamp. Seeing that this stranger had stolen the show.

It takes about fifteen more minutes to get started. That night, the protocols went out the window. In order not to delay the event any longer, Martinez did not present George's presentation; he only tried to explain to himself how a candidate for governor of Florida had become the center of a scandal and the end of his political career, if that so call red beard Viking appears with lawyers the next day seeking for the permits to use of the city hall.

George, as an experienced politician, tries to disguise his anger and begins his speech by thanking everyone present and takes advantage of the incident.

"Today, we definitely made history. Not only because I proclaim my candidacy for the presidency of the United States before you, but because we have started with an unfortunate incident that caused the delay of our meeting by almost an hour. This incident was based on a misunderstanding, but thanks to that misunderstanding I could see that there is a thriving youth determined to fight for what they believe is right. For me, it is the motivation to keep fighting for a better future. "

The audience applauds him loudly, and they stand up. George to win over Nick invites him to go on the podium.

Nick is not used to standing in front of the audience, so he tries to evade the situation, but George sees it as a weak point and capitalizes on him.

"Please, it would be a snub to me and these students that we have seen in you the material of a future leader."

The students stand up and start screaming, raising their right arms. "THE VIKING, THE VIKING" Nick looked like a tomato with red hair and red beard. Mark and Roberto take him by the arms and make him stand. Nick, with stage fright, walks to the podium and stands two feet away from George, who seeks more sympathy from the audience. George puts his arm arround him and basically drags him to the podium in front of the microphone.

"Tell us your name, please."

Nick, with his gaze totally down without looking at the audience, responds.

"Nicholas Field."

"What kind of work do you do?"

"I have a small mechanical workshop."

George, seeing Nick's shy attitude, tortured him with a few more questions. Nick looked like an embarrassed student answering questions, his eyes fixed on George's notes reading them, trying to figure out how long the event would be. When George had satisfied himself by torturing Nick and destroying the student's hero, he said.

"Thank you, Nick. Go back to your seat, please."

Nick was walking to his seat with his head down, and George gave him the last lunge. "I ask for a round of applause for our Viking."

Only Mark, Roberto, and George applauded until Nick took his place. George felt he had not only defeated the Viking but also sunk his ship to prevent him from returning. For the next two hours, Nick didn't hear a word of what George said. He just thought about the ridicule he had made.

He knew that the regulation that limited the number of occupants in a room was true, so he gave the commissioner the benefit of a doubt. Nick wakes up from his trance when the audience applauds loudly. Nick stands up too and clap not even knowing why he was clapping for.

When everyone sits down, George says. "I know you all have questions. It is impossible for me to answer all your questions. I will take seven random questions to answer, but I want you to know that I will answer all questions you send to my email."

Mark stands up and says. "I have a question for you."

George looks at him and replies. "I think I've been very clear about the procedure. If I choose your question, I will answer it right here and if I don't choose your question, I will answer it by email."

Mark angrily replies. "You just fear my question."

People say. "HUUUU!!!" George reacted immediately to the HUUUU!!! shout.

"Young man, you are disrespectful, but ask your question." George responds angrily.

"This administration has had many failures and you have never criticized it. Why should I vote for you, which is the continuation of the old problems?"

George stares at him and asks. "Were you in the military?"

"No, and that doesn't answer my question."

George persuasively responds.

"For a person like you, it doesn't answer it, but that's the basis of the answer. I belong to a party, to an administration and mainly to the people. An army cannot win a battle if soldiers do not carry out orders simply because they do not share it, that crumbles morale and makes victory impossible. It is the same case in politics. I am a soldier loyal to my party and my administration. I agree that we have made mistakes. But who hasn't done them? That does not give me the right, nor would it bring anything positive if I disqualify the effort of others. In our private meetings, we present different criteria, but we must give a sense of unity and firmness before the world when leaving those meetings. Just as in the army, follow the orders and move up the ranks if you want to change things. That's why I'm here to look for a better future without destroying the present and if you want a change, then help me change things or you should run to change it yourself."

George's response was so clear and forceful that even Mark himself applauded him. George had shown that he was in control, not only defeated the Viking and sank the ship. Within an hour, he had just given the deadly lunge to the last survivor of the Viking ship.

"If I may now, I will answer the questions from the audience."

A child approaches the podium with a basket full of folded papers. George takes one he opens it and puts it on the podium next to his notes and says.

"Someone asks me. Why vote for you? I think it's a pretty similar question, but with a different approach than the one I just answered."

While George gave an elaborate answer, Nick remembered seeing that question on the podium note list. Nick thought it was a common question, even Mark asked it, so he credited George for his readiness and his sympathy for him increased. George ended with his answer, and they applauded him again. The boy returns with the basket of questions and George takes out another piece of paper, puts it on the podium as if he read it, moves his head affirmatively.

"This is an interesting question; I am pleased that we have a thinking and worried audience about the future. Someone asks. Where should we invest more, in industry or education? "

When Nick heard the question, he remembered it. Nick saw the question written on George's notes. Nick accepted the first, but the second would be too much. He jabbed his elbow into Mark. Mark was excited as a child watching a fantasy movie. "That man is a son of a bitch."

Mark thought Nick had said it as flattery and responds.

"Yes, he is. We need a son of a bitch like him in the White House."

Roberto looks at them and answers. "Well, sell it to someone else because I don't buy him."

Nick remained silent, but he swore he would make him pay for the embarrassment George had made him go through in front of the audience. Nick was about to explode and prepared for battle. Never in his life had he had a day with so many emotions. When George finishes answering the sixth question, Nick tells Mark and Roberto.

"Be prepared that the party is going to start now. I'm going to make him pay for everything that asshole did to me."

George takes the seventh paper in the basket and before he reads it, Nick stands up and says.

"Mr. Senator, I am sorry to interrupt you, but I would like to ask you a favor before you read the question."

One student screams as a joke. "The Viking is resurrecting." This comment produces laughter in the audience and George, trying to finish at once, responds. "Gladly friend, I am here to serve you."

Nick stands and speaks loudly enough for the entire audience to hear. "I know a person who invests in the stock market. He tells me he can triple my money and asks me to put my savings in his hands. I am afraid because it is my family's savings. It is not money that is left over. The worst thing about it is that I have discovered that this man is dishonest and often deceives those who have placed their trust in him. What do you advise me?"

Mark and Roberto looked at each other in total bewilderment, while they heard some taunts from the audience. George calls for silence and responds in a Solomonic way.

"NEVER", I repeat, "NEVER" give your money or your friendship to a dishonest person, because in the end you will lose money and the friendship. Honesty is the fundamental basis for any type of relationship or business. And be very careful, because the dishonest person is the one who most boasts of honesty. You were lucky to find out in time and not put your trust in him, because I am sure that others have not had that same luck. "

Nick applauds, and the audience doesn't react. There's no applause or teasing; it's as if they know it's the beginning of something interesting.

Nick turns around and confronts the audience. His anger was such that he lost the stage fright that two hours ago caused his humiliation.

"I want you to know that the senator's words are true and wise, he just needs to say that the one who lies in small things also lies in the big things and that a dishonest person thinks others will not find out because they are stupid or are at a much lower level."

Nick turns around and heads to George. "Isn't this a true senator?"

George reddens. Something is being plotted by the Viking. He was not as dead as he thought. "Yes, you are right, and I think you are abusing my time and the patience of the audience. Please take a seat and let me end with the seventh question. Then I'm going to invite you and your friends for dinner and you can ask me whatever you want all night."

"Thank you, but I shouldn't get together with dishonest people based on your own advice. Regarding the next question, save yourself the work of reading it. I will tell you what it is: "Will you choose a male vice president or a female vice president?" You have answered none of the questions from the audience. You have seven dummies in the audience who will get up as if they wrote the questions. Those questions you have them written in your notes. When you took me to the podium, I looked down and saw those questions written in your notes. You are a fake."

George slaps the podium and yells at him. "Enough! Get out of the auditorium."

All the students and a few more in the audience started screaming. Some shouted "Viking" others shouted "FAKE." Martinez called the sergeant over the radio, who was already entering with the security guard, attracted by the screams of the public. The security guard tells him. "Oh no! The fucking Viking again."

The sergeant who was a resentful Trump's sympathizer took it personal on this occasion. Before the sergeant could ask, George tells him.

"I want you to take this individual out of the room. He not only interrupts the event, but he has had the audacity to offend me in front of the audience. And I want you to know that I'm going to sue you for defamation. There is a big difference between freedom of speech and defamation. I will not let any madman stain my reputation and laugh about it."

Nick responds. "I invite you to sue me. I would love you to do it. I said it and I repeat it, you are a liar, and the proof is in your notes and the seven pieces of paper that you have on the podium. And since you are going to enter litigation, the sergeant must collect evidence."

The confused sergeant asks. " What evidence are you talking about?"

Nick is pointing towards the podium. "In his notes, he has written the questions that he answered and the papers that he supposedly read have other questions, that is part of the evidence, also the six people of the public who stood up when he read the questions must appear in court under oath of perjury."

The students prevented two of the people posing as the writers of the questions from leaving the room. Martinez is on the verge of fainting, and George doesn't know what to do.

The sergeant realizes Nick has caught the senator red-handed and climbs to the podium. George orders him with character.

"What are you doing here? I called you to get that guy out of the room."

The sergeant, in a calm voice and enjoying the stage, responds.

"I will do it immediately, but first I should collect your notes as evidence."

"What evidence? That will be a civil case. You don't have to get involved, plus I don't think it's worth wasting my time in court during a campaign. I won't bring up any charges."

The audience began booing the senator on all sides of the room.

Nick screams. "You won't sue, but I will, so I need those papers."

The sergeant felt enormous satisfaction, so many marches in vain in favor of Trump and now it is his was turn to laugh. "Senator, I need your notes, please."

The senator lifts the notes with his right hand and puts it out of the sergeant's reach. "I will gladly give them to you if you get a court order, because they are private property."

George did not realize that he had left the six papers of the alleged questions exposed and the sergeant, with a blow of a snake attack, took them.

"What are you doing? That's not yours. Give it to me right now." The senator shouted.

The Sergeant, undeterred, responds. "It's not yours either. This is from the public and it's the evidence that exonerates you of all guilt. Or not?"

George, in a last desperate attempt, approaches him and mutters.

"If you destroy me. You will spend the rest of your career covering your backs, but if you help me, I will promote you to captain."

The sergeant responds in the same tone of voice. "How can you assure me of something like that? What guarantee do I have that you will keep your word?"

George responds. "My connections go beyond what you can imagine, plus I know you have me recorded on your body camera. What else do you want from me?"

The sergeant responds mockingly. "Yes, I want something else. I want you to know that you're being placed under arrest for trying to bribe the authority and that now I don't need a warrant for your fucking notes."

The sergeant speaks loudly and close to the microphone, making his words heard by all. "Senator George Martin, you are under arrest for trying to bribe a law enforcement officer."

Despite the screams of the audience, the sergeant read him his rights, but not even with a hundred amplifiers they could hear a word. Martinez ran to the podium. "What do you do? Have you gone crazy? How are you going to arrest a senator? Who the fuck do you think you are?"

The sergeant, undeterred, responds to him. "Commissioner, what makes you believe that if I arrest a senator of the nation, I will lack the courage to arrest a county commissioner? This is my only and final warning. Please step aside, or I will arrest you for obstruction of justice."

Martinez understands that it's in his best interest to step aside before it's too late for him. The police responded to the call related to the arrest of the senator and in just a few minutes, many reporters, police officers and politicians entered the room without asking for an entrance ticket or worrying about the regulation of the fire department.

The news was on the front page of all the newspapers of the nation The New York Times titled it "DEBUT AND FAREWELL" the Washington Post "Who is the Red Beard Viking?" and The Miami Herald said, "The state of Florida increasingly dangerous: ALIGATORS, ANACONDAS, BEARS and now VIKINGS."

CHAPTER THREE

Meeting with Barry Johnson.

In the city of Atlanta, Georgia, Texas Republican Senator Barry Johnson celebrated the disaster of Senator George Martin's opening campaign.

"Gentlemen, the polls gave Senator George Martin as the most complete candidate within the ranks of the Democratic Party for the electoral contest. It will take them a while to decide which of the other six candidates they will support for the race. Ha, Ha, Ha, the Titanic sank on opening night."

Barry's assistant says. "Senator, I think we should wait for Florida to cool down a bit. If we go to Florida right now, they will talk about George and not talk about us."

"I agree, but tell Eugene to find out everything he can about that Viking. We must use it to our advantage. People like improvised leaders and a lot more when they are local. I also want Eugene to tell the lawyer to investigate if George followed the protocol to rent the Miami City Hall. If they were doing the meeting without the city authorization, that will be the end of George. Also, make sure we follow the protocol; we can't make the same mistake they made."

Meanwhile, it was a surprise for Nick when he left home for work in the morning to be ambushed by four reporters.

"Can you please tell us your name?" A reporter asks.

"What motivates you to get involved in politics?" Another reporter.

Nick responds. "I'm not a politician. I'm not interested in politics, but I also don't like to be seen as stupid, that's all."

Nick dodges reporters and retreats in his car in a hurry. Brittany, Nick's wife, is a young woman in her thirties with brown hair, white skin, and blue eyes. She realizes her husband had left and forgot the juice she had prepared for him. Brittany comes out with the juice in her hands wearing a house robe and only with the beauty that Mother Nature had given her, since she had only brushed her teeth. Brittany does not know what had happened the night before with her husband and upon hearing her husband's car, she hurried out, calling him. "Nick, Nick, Nick."

The four reporters and two cameramen turn around and run toward Brittany. Brittany, frightened, drops the juice and runs in a hurry inside the house, slamming the door so hard that the welcome sign fell to the ground.

She was not the only one that was taken by surprise, Commissioner Martinez. Martinez had taken a different path to avoid reporters, but failed. A reporter from the Miami Herald takes him by surprise.

"What is your opinion about what happened yesterday at city hall?"

"I have no words to express how embarrassed I am before my constituents. Senator George Martin's behavior has broken all the rules and betrayed our trust. To some extent, I'm glad, since this clarified that Floridians more than partisanship want honesty."

"Were the protocols for renting the town hall followed?"

"I wish I could answer that question, but I don't have the answer. I delegated that task to my assistant. I was extremely busy with the organization and the logistics of Senator George Martin's meeting; that include the accommodation, transportation and security of the senator. I am afraid that based on the inexperience of this young man, there may be irregularities. That does not mean that the young man acted with malice. He is a nineteen-year-old with a lot of desire to serve and little experience. I ask you please not to destroy the future of a bright young man like him."

Thanks to the free publicity received by the local and national media, Nick's shop increased its clientele, but it ceased to be Nicholas' shop and became the red beard Viking shop.

Eugene communicates with Senator Barry in Washington as they had agreed. "Good morning, Senator, today marks two weeks since there has been no comment about the incident, nor they have mentioned the Viking by any means. What is the step to follow now?"

"Very well, Eugene, contact Miami Commissioner Juan Otero to make the arrangements. I want to launch my election campaign in the same place, but I want everything by the book and there can be no entrance tickets. I will make it on a first-come, first-served basis."

Eugene interrupts. "Senator, if we do it like that, we cannot control who enters and they can sabotage the event."

"That's why the radio should broadcast that the doors will open at half past seven, but you will tell all our guests that the entrance will be at half-past five." Answers Barry.

Eugene worriedly replies. "Senator, that's very early."

"Not Eugene. Remember that the vast majority are Cubans and if you say at half-past six, they will show up at half past seven. We cannot take any risks. I also want you to invite the Viking with his friends and Sergeant Stanley. They will be my guests of honor in the front row."

Eugene responds. "I will do so, Senator, but Sergeant Stanley retired from the police force a week after the incident. According to my contacts, they offered him a full pension as a captain, but on the clause that he could never talk about it. Since he had twenty-seven years of service, he didn't think twice about accepting it."

"It doesn't matter. Their presence is enough to show support. Remember that I want forty percent of the public to be black, so you pick up as many Haitians as you can."

Eugene asked worriedly. "Senator, what's the purpose of filling the town hall with Haitians if the vast majority do not have papers?"

"Eugene, you have been working for fifteen years with me. It's time for you to see beyond your nose. We need the black vote; the cameras can't distinguish between a Haitian and an African American. The African Americans will believe that we have their support and that will motivate them to vote for us."

Otero and Eugene got to work immediately; in just two weeks, they would have to prepare the campaign inauguration event. One morning, Otero shows up at Nick's business. "Good morning, Mr. Nicholas"

Nick takes off his thick glasses and wipes the sweat with the sleeve of his right hand, then puts them on. "Good morning. How can I help you? "

"I am Miami City Commissioner Juan Otero. Texas Republican Senator Barry Johnson has asked me to invite you and your two friends to the inauguration of his campaign next Friday. You are his guests of honor."

Mark and Roberto had heard the conversation, so Mark instantly replies.

"It will be an honor; we will be there."

Nick and Roberto look at Mark, who understands he shouldn't have gotten into the conversation.

Roberto responds. "Don't count on me. I'm not a politician or anyone's puppet. I'm very old to be taken as an asshole. If you and Mark want to go, then good luck. I rather to go to bed early."

Mark replies. "Grandpa, don't be such a party-pooper. You had fun last time and now you don't want to go."

"I'm not fucking going." Roberto responds with a bad temper.

Nick steps in. "Enough, if he doesn't want to go, he doesn't go. No one is going to force him. Politics always brings problems and arguments between friends. Here you are the only one who talks about politics and there have never been problems because we do not listen to you."

Otero, trying to ingratiate himself with Nick, responds.

"Wise words, Mr. Nicholas, politics is not for everyone, even though it affects us all. Anyway, we will keep a place for you in case you change your mind."

Nick responds. "What did you tell me your name was?"

"Commissioner Juan Otero, but you can call me Otero."

Nick wipes the sweat from his forehead again and responds.

"Please tell the senator that I thank him, but that I will not attend. After that event, for four days, the reporters were fucking with me wherever I went. "

Otero shakes Nick's hand as a farewell and then puts his left hand on Nick's shoulder. "What you just told me reminds me of a very famous passage from the book, "DON QUIXOTE DE LA MANCHA," and that passage comes to you like a ring to your finger."

Nick, intrigued, replies. "Yes, what is it?"

Otero responds. "Don Quixote rode on his horse and Sancho Panza rode on his donkey. Sancho tells

Don Quixote," Lord, the dogs are barking at us" and Don Quixote replied. "That means we are moving, Sancho." So, if those reporters bark at you, that means you're being moving and noticed by many people, so I hope you don't stop moving. Have a good afternoon and here I leave my card for anything I can help you with."

Those words took effect on Nick, who did not respond and kept the card in his pocket. Otero contacts the senator and informs him that everything is prepared and that the only thing that is not confirmed is the attendance of the Viking and one of his friends. The senator responds slowly but firm.

"I don't care if the two friends of the fucking Viking disappear from the earth, but you talk to the governor of Florida and tell him to give the shitty Viking a call and convince him. Remember that the jerk has become popular and that attracts a lot of votes. We should capitalize on that."

The next day Nick is doing an oil change to a car when the phone rings. Nick looks and sees that Roberto is changing a tire, and Mark is working in the air of another car. Nick sees Mark is the one closest to the phone and yells at him. "Mark, can you answer that call, please?"

Mark gets out of the car and goes to answer the call, suddenly puts the receiver aside and runs to Nick.

"Nick, Nick, the governor is on the line and wants to talk to you."

Nick, thinking Mark is playing a prank on him, takes the oil filter and moves like if he is going to throw it at him. "Stop it, make fun of your own mother."

Mark says, "Nick, I am serious. The governor is on the line and wants to talk to you."

Nick goes to answer the phone, but he doesn't believe that the governor is on the line. He picks up the phone and says. "Nick speaking. How can I help you?"

"Good afternoon, Mr. Nicholas Field, this is Florida Governor Harry Lake, your governor speaking. How are you?"

Nick felt a chill all over his body. It was true. What was going on? Why me? He takes a deep breath, counts to three, and responds.

"Good afternoon Mr. Governor, what a pleasure. What can I do for you?"

"The pleasure is mine. I wanted to call you three days ago, but I have been very busy. I just want to ask you to join us at the inauguration of Senator Barry Johnson's presidential campaign. We want you with us."

Nick doesn't know what to say. He scratches his head with his left hand while kicking into the wall. The governor, seeing that Nick does not answer his question.

"Nick, are you listening? Are you still there?"

"Yes governor, I hear you. It's that I have several commitments for this weekend; I don't want to say that I am going and then don't show up."

The governor tries a new strategy to convince him.

"You'll always will be fine with me, but the students want to see you again and Senator Barry Johnson also wants you by his side. You mean a lot to them; we will pick you up if necessary and drag you along. "

Nick was silent, kicking the wall harder and harder. The governor breaks the silence. "Nick, don't take it literally. No one is going to drag you anywhere. It's just that we hope you honor us with your presence. Thank you for your time."

Nick hangs up the phone angrily yells at Mark. "This is all your fault. You made us go to the event and look at the shit you've gotten me into. I'm not going anywhere."

Roberto approaches and advises him. "Yes, you must attend, Nick."

"Why, if I'm not interested in politics?"

Roberto says to him in a low voice. "Because when you went the first time, you made a lot of enemies in the county government and if you don't attend the second time, you will make more enemies, but this time at the state level. Just by attending, your enemies will not touch you because none of them wants problems with the governor of the state. Otherwise, you will be showered with fines and violations of all types."

Mark steps in. "Grandpa is right, and the devil knows more because of his age than for being the devil."

Nick angrily tells him. "Go to hell. I don't want to see your face."

Mark and Roberto can't help laughing. Mark turns around and retreats, imitating the students by jumping and screaming; "THE VIKING, THE VIKING."

Otero had convinced the students to take part in the event, which they had only accepted because Otero had promised them that the Viking would go with them. Otero told them he would pick them up in a van and then pick up the Viking with his friends. The students make a huge Viking helmet with its two huge horns and placed it on the roof of the van. When Otero saw the Viking helmet made by the students, he thought it was a good idea because that way it would be easier to convince Nick to take part. Otero was sure that Nick would not snub the students and would attend. Eugene had recruited some forty-five Haitians from the most marginal and needy areas. Eugene had promised them a gift card worth a hundred dollars and if they showed enthusiasm, he would give them an additional card for two hundred dollars.

Roberto hears a car horn playing in front of the shop and goes out to investigate. Roberto sees the van with the huge Viking helmet and says.

"Oh my God, what the hell is that? Nick! Nick! Come out here, they are looking for you."

Nick leaves the office and is speechless. The students led by Brandon were already inside the shop with Otero.

Nick, totally surprised, tells them.

"Have you guys gone crazy?"

Brandon, believing that Nick had given his word to attend the event, responds.

"Of course, we are crazy with joy, knowing that you would attend; we could not miss out this one. What do you think of the helmet we made for you?"

Otero sees Nick doesn't know what to answer and says. Senator Barry and Governor Harry have reserved the front seats for you, your friends, and the students Roberto puts his hand on Nick's shoulder and whispers.

"You must attend. You have no alternative."

Nick, looking for an excuse, answers, "I'm not dressed to attend any event."

Brandon, with a smile which is truly sincere, responds.

"That doesn't matter. What matters is your presence. In addition, you represent the working class that suffers and needs a change. You have proven to have principles and leadership. That is why we are here, and we will not take no for an answer."

Otero takes advantage of the students and tells Nick.

"Don't do it for the senator or the governor, do it for these guys. They don't deserve to be despised by you."

Nick looks at Roberto, who moves his head affirmatively. Nick looks out and sees Mark already at the door of the van, signaling Nick to come in. Roberto pushes Nick in the back and tells him.

"Go with them Nick. I close the business."

Brandon shakes Roberto's hand and says. "Thank you, grandpa, I promise you we will take care of him."

The senator and the governor were at the entrance of the town hall to receive their guests, who were mainly wealthy donors. Eugene had arranged two school buses full of Haitians. They were parked about fifty feet from the entrance of city hall, and Eugene reminded them that the main thing was to show enthusiasm and applaud loudly, even if they don't understand what the senator was saying.

The Haitians had carried drums, but since they were at the end of the group, Eugene had not noticed them.

The senator is being interviewed next to the governor at the door of the town hall when Otero arrives with the van and the students. The students are singing the famous Queen song "WE ARE THE CHAMPIONS."

The Haitians, seeing the van with the big helmet and hearing the students singing, think that it is part of the game and they run towards the van shouting and playing their drums. Reporters, seeing what was happening, leave the senator and governor and begin recording live the triumphal entrance of the Viking being carried on the shoulder by the students and surrounded by a crowd singing and playing drums. The students did not notice the senator and the governor at the entrance of the town hall and the Haitians did not know who the senator and the governor standing at the entrance were. The senator and governor had to step aside to avoid being run over by the crowd.

When the crowd entered the town hall, the senator and the governor saw Otero and Eugene approaching, who tried to avoid such a spectacle, to no avail. The senator loses control and tells them.

"What the fuck have you guys done? Have you brought that clown to steal the event? It is not enough that this asshole became a celebrity at the Democratic event. Now I will have to mention him and increase his fame. That happens to me for trusting a couple of stupid idiots. Get out of my face. I don't want to see you. Get out."

Eugene and Otero looked at each other and left in a hurry. The Senator was so furious that he had not noticed that a reporter with his camera had recorded his screams and insults. The governor, trying to calm the senator and tells him. "Calm down. Your anger can make you make mistakes, and we can't afford that luxury. I am sure that within the reporters, there will be those who are looking for that moment to capitalize on it."

Barry takes a deep breath and responds. "You're absolutely right. I must smile at the audience and jokingly take the Viking's antics to lessen his importance."

The town hall was at full capacity. Senator Barry begins by thanking the political figures for organizing the event and then the donors of his campaign who were present. Barry points to Haitians and says. "I'm glad to see the vigorous support that the African American community gives us. I want to tell you I identify with your problems, which will be my priority when I become president."

Barry knows he can't overlook Nick after such an entrance and sitting in the front row. Against his will and pulling out a forced smile, Barry points to Nick and says. "I can't overlook our Viking."

When the Haitians saw Senator Barry point to Nick and say Viking, they stood up and clapped loudly and play their singing drums; "VIKING, VIKING." The students joined in, standing up and applauding loudly. The remaining audience looked at each other without knowing what to do. Some in the audience thought Senator Barry planned it and stood up, applauding Nick. This caused the rest of the audience to join in and they all ended up standing, applauding Nick.

The senator couldn't believe what was going on. He reddened, and his blood pressure rose to a somewhat dangerous point. Barry, so that the audience did not see his angry face, turns around, looking towards the invited politicians who were sitting behind him. The politicians, seeing Barry's angry face, think Barry has become angry at them for sitting around when they are all standing clapping and shouting "VIKING." They all stand up and start applauding.

Senator Barry is about to faint, hits the podium hard and screams.

"Enough is enough, enough, I said enough."

Everyone sits down, listening to Senator Barry's screams. Obviously, many were disgusted because Barry had yelled at them as if they were spoiled children. Barry understands he has made another mistake by yelling at the audience. He does not know how to amend the situation. Everything is going from bad to worse. Senator Barry tries to start his speech, but his blood pressure has risen to a serious point and Barry says many inconsistencies without realizing it. No one dares to say anything, and his speech is a mess.

Haitians were worrying, Eugene had promised to give them a visa card worth a hundred dollars at the start of the event and to give them another one for the same value after the event was over. Eugene had told them he would sit with them and be there until the end to give them the other card. The Haitians comment among themselves that they believe Eugene has deceived them because one of them said he saw Eugene leave before the event began.

To end his event, Senator Barry answers questions.

"I will not take papers or have questions prepared from anyone. I will answer your concerns without hesitation."

Barry was sweating and constantly wiping his glasses without realizing that his eyesight was clouding, and it wasn't due to dirty lenses. One of the Haitians who half spoke English tells the group. "If this is over, we won't see any money. We have to ask where Eugene is."

The Haitian stands up and says out loud. "I have a question."

Senator Barry moves his head in the affirmative and responds.

"I know the African American community has a lot of questions, and I have the answers. Tell me your name and what your question is."

The Haitian responds with a strong accent.

"My name Pier Batiste. Me want to know where is Eugene?"

The question is so out of place that it causes laughter to all in the audience, except for the senator who angrily answers it.

"This is a serious event, much more than you imagine. Do you have a question or not?"

Pier responds, a little angry as well. "Eugene brought us here and promised us he would be here until the end, and they told me he was gone."

The senator, who knew nothing of the agreement between Eugene and the Haitians, responds.

"Sorry buddy, but Eugene left a long time ago. You'll have to see him another day."

Pier's enraged screams. "Then who is going to pay us? You have seen the faces of idiots; I want my money."

The senator can no longer stand it, his sight becomes increasingly cloudy. Pier, with his imposing size, goes forward and points to Nick and says.

"If Eugene doesn't pay us, then you pay us, because he told us you would be here, and that we had to applaud for you."

Nick gets up from his chair enraged and before he could say a word already had three microphones in front of his face.

"You are wrong friend; I would never buy votes or sell mine. If anyone gets any benefit from such a fraud, it must be some politician. But I'm so glad this happened to you, so you learn you cannot trust a politician if he is buying your vote."

Nick points to the senator and the politicians behind the senator.

"You have turned our state into a banana republic. I hope that the weight of the law will fall on all those who are implicated in this fraud. I also want you to know that there are many of us who believe in democracy and the values of our constitution. Nobody will use me as a trophy, much less for dirty campaigns. I do not lend myself to deceive the people. I am part of the people and I suffer with the people. How can a person chosen by his people engage them so miserably? Finally, I want the corrupted to be reminded that what is done in the dark will come to light, eventually. "

Brandon screams. "Long live the Viking." "The Viking for President."

They had diverted all attention to Nick, and no one noticed that Senator Barry was bent and about to fall to the floor. Barry falls to the floor fainting, and that's when everyone runs to help and he is rushed to Jackson Memorial Hospital.

Nick made national news again the New York Time writes, "Miami becomes a graveyard for politicians." Washington Post writes. "The Viking destroys Democrats and Republicans alike." The Miami Herald writes. "Will we have a Viking president?"

CHAPTER FOUR

The trail.

Nick became a national celebrity, but more for his controversial character than as a political figure. His stance had only brought him enemies from all political sides who sought revenge and to send a message to anyone who wanted to imitate him.

For a week, reporters would surprise Nick and his wife, trying to find some comment that would allow them to continue the saga and sell their newspapers. Brandon, Namir and Victor were the three most politically active law students. Brandon was the leader of the student's team and was aware of the harassment Nick was suffering at the hands of politicians. They saw in Nick a potential candidate and gave him a visit to his shop. Nick was in his office when he saw a red Volkswagen Beatle parked with a Viking helmet in his parking lot. Nick sees the students get out of the car and puts his hands on his head and says.

"My God, please. What do these guys want now?"

The students enter the office and Nick greets them cordially. Each gives Nick a big hug and Brando tells him.

"We bring you a present, and we want you to put it in your office."

Brando gives him a present wrapped in wrapping paper. Nick takes it and answers. "Thank you, guys, you shouldn't bother."

Namir takes her cell phone and starts recording the moment. Victor tells him to open it and if he doesn't like it, they will change it for another. Nick opens the gift and sees a wall clock shaped like the head of a Viking with his helmet and their respective horns. Nick laughs, thanks him and gives him a big hug. Brandon tells Nick.

"We would like to ask you to let us choose the place where to put it. We do not want it to be hidden. We want your customers to see it, so they know who you are and that when you look at it, you remember us."

Nick feels committed and accepts that the students choose the place. The students looked for the right place and finally put it on the side wall where everyone who entered or was inside had to see the clock.

Brandon, before saying goodbye to Nick, tells him. "We believe you can be a good political candidate."

Nick laughs and raises his arms. "No thanks, I don't even know how I have fallen into this, but the only thing I have achieved is to get enemies from on all sides. This month alone, I have to go to court twice to defend myself against a speeding ticket and then I have to defend myself against a violation of the county code. I've had to put cameras inside my car to record both my speed and the encounter with the officers. That has saved me from tickets, because seeing that I am recording them, they take another attitude and give me any stupid excuse for the stop. I must also say that many have stopped me to congratulate me and offer me help in case I needed it."

Victor tells Nick. "Remember that we have many connections, and we are at your service. It is very difficult to beat a traffic officer. It is your word against theirs and if they use a radar, not even God can save you. "

Nick smiles and responds. "That's also what the officer believes, but I have prepared a surprise for him. I know how to defend myself, especially when it is an injustice. The day of the traffic trail probably will be his last day at work."

The students looked at each other; they knew Nick was a box of surprises, so they attended court that day to support him. On the day of the trial, the fifteen students plus eight more students showed up to support Nick.

The magistrate calls Nick's case and Nick sands stands up. The traffic officer stands up and says. "Officer Rene Otero representing the state."

The judge turns to Nick and tells him.

"You have been fined for speeding, driving sixty-five miles per hour in a thirty-five zone. How do plead?"

Nick responds. "Not guilty, your Honor."

The judge turns to the officer and tells him. "Officer, let me hear your testimony."

The officer showing arrogance responds.

"On March second at approximately 7:25 PM, I was at the intersection of Le Jeune Road and southwest Eighth Street facing in a southbound direction, waiting for the traffic light to change. The light changed to yellow for eastbound and westbound traffic on Eighth Street. The defendant sped up, trying to pass the intersection before the light changed to red. The traffic light turned red when the defendant was in the middle of the intersection. I turned right to follow the defendant and followed him for about a minute. I wanted to give him the benefit of the doubt, thinking that the defendant would slow down after passing the interception, but he still didn't slow down. I had the defendant's vehicle in front of my patrol car with no obstruction, so I used my radar to determine his speed. The radar gave a reading of sixty-five miles per hour. I turned on my overhead lights and stopped the defendant at the above-mentioned location. The defendant provided me with his driver license, vehicle registration and insurance. After checking the defendant's record, I issued him a speeding citation. All this occurred in the City of Miami Dade County, Florida."

The officer picks up a folder and says. "Here is the logbook with the radar calibration that shows that it is up to date in case the defendant or your Honor wants to review it."

The Judge turns to Nick and tells him. "Your turn Mr. Field. What is your defense?"

"Your Honor, if I lie to the court. What would be the consequences?"

The annoying judge responds. "If you lie to the court, I assure you that you will be very sorry and that you will spend a few days in jail. Any other questions?

Nick moves his head in the affirmative and responds.

"And if the officer is the one lying. Will he receive the same treatment?"

Huuuu! A big murmur is felt in the courtroom and the angry judge says.

"Mr. Field, I am aware of who you are and your track record. I assure you I will not allow you to turn my court into another of your theaters. If that's what you have to say, then I'll find you guilty."

Nick responds immediately. "Not it is the other way around. I have a lot to say, only that I would like to give the officer the opportunity to retract his testimony. I would not like his career to be ruined."

The officer interrupts and says. "Your Honor, the defendant obviously believes that he can manipulate the court based on his ridiculous notoriety. That day, I could give him a fine for speeding, a fine for accelerating to pass on yellow and another fine for running the red light. When I realized who the defendant was, to avoid this spectacle, I gave him only one fine, but it was worthless, because the defendant believes that he is above the law."

Nick turns to the judge and responds. "Your Honor, when I finish, you will determine who here is the one who you think is above the law."

The judge responds. "I've heard enough, and you didn't say anything, I find you guilty."

Nick responds. "You have not heard my defense; I have the right to my defense."

The judge looks at him furiously and, being sure that Nick has no defense, responds.

"OK, go ahead, be brief and to the point."

Nick pointing to the officer responds.

"First, the officer was coming after me. He wasn't where he said he was. I never enter the interception at that speed or pass with the red light."

Nick turns to the officer and says. "It isn't true what I just said, officer?"

Officer Otero opens his arms and says. "Your Honor, is it necessary to listen to this?"

Before the judge says a word, Nick says.

"That is the reason the officer does not bring the photo of the intersection cameras, because they would show the opposite of his testimony. The officer's other big lie is that he followed me for about a minute when I was supposedly traveling at sixty-five miles per hour. If that was true, it would put me at more than a mile west of the interception, when in fact he stopped me less than a third of a mile from intercession as written on the ticket. That evidence exposes Officer Otero."

The enraged judge turns to the officer and, almost screaming, says.

"Officer Otero, what do you have to say about it?"

The officer is uncovered and doesn't know what to say and reddens like a tomato.

The judge, seeing that the officer was not responding, turns to Nick and says. "You have something else to add, Mr. Field."

"Yes, your Honor, my contacts informed me that Officer Otero is the brother of Commissioner Juan Otero who blames me for being discredited for fraudulent conduct during Senator Barry's event. Commissioner Otero said he would make my life impossible and that I would have to leave the state of Florida. I was born here, and I do not flee from the threats of any corrupt politician."

Everyone in the room stands up and applauds excitedly. The judge tries to bring order to the room even though he wanted to join the applause. The order finally returns to the courtroom, and the judge says.

"Mr. Field, your charges are dismissed. I congratulate you on such a brilliant defense."

Then the judge goes to Otero. "Officer Otero, you are an embarrassment to your department. You will be detained for falsifying evidence and lying to the court."

The court officer escorts Officer Otero out of the courtroom and takes him into custody.

Nick is back making news. The Miami Herald put the photo of Officer Otero with the headline: "One more victim of the Viking." The New York Time wrote: "Will anyone dare to go against the Viking?" After Officer Otero's arrest, the harassment of Nick decreased dramatically, but Nick did not lower his guard and kept cameras in his car to record any incidents. Three weeks of relative calm passed, and Nick kept busy in his shop, as the clientele increased because of Nick's popularity.

Nick returns to court, and this time the group of students had doubled. Nick, without realizing it, had become the student's leader. When Nick enters the courtroom, he is surprised to see the students. The room was at full capacity, even reporters were waiting outside the room as no cameras or microphones were allowed in the room. The judge was an African American known for her bad temper and righteousness. The judge was aware of Nick's controversial figure and when it was Nick's turn she started saying.

"Mr. Field, I am aware of your record, and I want to warn you that under no circumstances will I allow you to turn my courtroom into a circus. You just answer the questions without getting off topic. Do you understand me?"

Nick feels scolded and uncomfortable with the judge's attitude, but decides not to answer. The judge says. " You are accused of not having your establishment in compliance with the county code, depriving disabled people of the conditions to access your establishment. How do you plead?"

Nick remains thoughtful and responds. "Do they have to testify if I plead guilty?"

The confused judge asks. "Who are they?"

Nick points out to the lawyer and his witness, who was a disabled person. The judge answers. "No, they don't have to testify, but if you plead not guilty, they will present their case and then you will defend yourself."

Nick responds. "In that case, I plead not guilty."

The judge turns to the lawyer and says. "Your testimony, please."

The lawyer shakes his head in a bewilderment manner and responds.

"If here the defendant wishes to make a circus of this court, he cannot. The evidence is clear and unquestionable."

The lawyer points to the witness and says. "On the eighth day of February, the witness seated here."

The witness tries to stand up, but the judge, seeing that the witness was missing his right leg, interrupts. "You don't have to stand up. Just say your name."

The witness says "Ramon Delgado, your Honor."

The lawyer continues. "As I said earlier, on the eighth of February, Mr. Ramon showed up at the defendant's business with his car at 9:30 AM to change the brakes pads. He parked, looked around and saw that he could not enter the office because it does not have the ramp required by law, nor was the office door wide enough for him to enter with his wheelchair. The witness, tired of his disability being ignored, not only by the defendant but by many other establishments, acted so that this situation is corrected. The witness does it, not only for him but for the many disabled like him who suffer from the same discrimination."

The lawyer takes some enlarged photographs and gives them to the court officer, who gives them to the judge.

"When the witness contacted me, I went to the defendant's premises to verify the veracity of the accusation. As you can see in the photos presented as evidence in court; not only does the office door have no entrance ramp, nor the width necessary for a disabled person to enter with their wheelchair, but also the bathroom does not have the right conditions for a disabled person to access the bathroom if they need it. "

The judge looks at the photos and gives them to the court officer, who gives them to Nick. The judge asks Nick. "Are those photos of your establishment?"

Nick responds. "Yes, those are photos of my business?"

The judge snarls into his eyes and points her finger at Nick.

"Then how dare you plead not guilty when you know that what the lawyer says is true?"

Nick says. "No, your Honor, the lawyer and the witness are lying. I have proof that they lie."

The angry judge responds. "How are you going to tell me they are lying if you yourself have told me that the photos are real?"

Nick takes out a pen drive out of his pocket and says. "Here is my evidence that shows they are lying to the court. This is the copy of the security cameras of the eighth day of February from 8:00 AM to 2:00 PM where you can see that the witness never went to my business. Even better, that the witness has had no vehicle registered in his name for three years. The witness uses the special shuttle service that the county offers to the disabled people to go to their medical appointments. The witness has not driven since he lost his leg in a terrible accident three years ago. A private investigator, who is present is in the room, will present the evidence to the court."

The enraged judge asks. "Where is that witness?"

The private investigator stands up and says. "Erick Kinderland, your Honor."

Erick picks up a folder with his right hand and says. "Here I have the evidence that proves the veracity of what the defendant said to the court."

The court officer takes the folder and hands it over to the judge. The judge examines the documents and closes it angrily. "Counsel, are you aware of this?"

The court officer takes the folder and hands it over to the lawyer. The lawyer takes the documents and puts on a surprised face.

"Your Honor, I was not aware of this earlier. The witness contacted me, and I went to check if what he had told me was true. I don't have to doubt the witness. I would never bring a case before the court, knowing that it is based on a lie from the start."

The judge says. "I understand." Then she looks at the witness who was extremely nervous and she saw his guilty face.

"Mr. Ramon, now you will have to stand up."

Ramon takes his crutch and stands up with his gaze fixed on the lawyer, who avoided eye contact with Ramon at all costs. The judge tells him.

"Look at me and forget about the counsel. You know that lies have short legs. You could lie to your lawyer, but not to the court. Lying under oath leads to fines, jail time, or both. I do not give privileges to disabled people who make a mockery of the judicial system, and I will punish you to the fullest that the law allows me to."

Ramon tells the lawyer. "You will not defend me; you will say nothing?"

The lawyer does not answer him, and Ramon angrily yells at him. "I'm talking to you don't play deaf."

The lawyer responds in a low voice. "This is a totally unrelated case to the one we came to today, but I will represent you and cover all the expenses of your defense. You don't have to worry."

Nick sees the judge believes the lawyer was not aware of what happened and raises his hand, asking for the floor.

The judge looks at him and answers. "What do you want now? Just because the witness lied, that doesn't exonerate you of the violation."

Nick calmly replies. "I agree with that."

The judge reluctantly tells him. "So, what, isn't it enough for you?"

Nick responds. "No, your Honor, there is much more behind this that you should know."

The judge leans back in her chair, puts her hand on her forehead and, knowing Nick's history, tries to appease him by telling him. "Oh my God! Isn't it enough for you that the witness goes to jail and receives a fine?"

Ramon heard what the judge said and saw that the lawyer ignored him and basically washed his hands. He says.

"Just a moment, your Honor. It is true that I never went to the Viking business."

The audience in the room laughed and even the judge covered her mouth to disguise that she was laughing.

Nick lowered his head and moved it from side to side and said. "Oh, my God! This Viking thing is going a lot further than what I thought."

Ramon continues. "I know the lawyer's wife. She told me that, if I testified in this trial, then through his contacts in the city, he would get me a low-income home. I accepted because I can hardly pay the rent of the room where I live. The lawyer contacted me and told me everything I needed to say to you. I told him that if he guaranteed me low-income housing, I would. He told me he guaranteed it and that's why I did. It was out of pure necessity."

The lawyer responds. "That's an infamy; I will sue you for defamation."

Ramon enraged at him. "You are a coward. Face the situation, be a man."

The judge gives three hammers on the table and puts order in the room. Nick tells the judge. "You will not blame me for this circus, even though I'm getting used to it."

The court bursts into laughter again and the judge lowers her head, but this time she can't hide her laughter. Nick tells the judge. "Laugh, laugh, but this is not over. I still have more."

The judge raised her hands in surrender. "No, no please, Mr. Field. I think it's enough."

Nick pointing towards the lawyer responds. "You must not know this. The lawyer who is representing the false witness is Maria Otero's husband."

The judge answers. "That has nothing to do with it here. Mrs. Maria Otero is not on trial. "

Nick continues. "Yes, but what you are not aware of is that the lawyer specializes in patents and contracts. He has never in his life represented anyone in a case like this. He also works as legal counsel for the City of Miami. His brother-in-law, Commissioner Juan Otero, blames me for his fall from grace during Senator Barry Johnson's event. Two weeks ago, Commissioner Otero's brother, Police Officer Rene Otero, was fired from the department for fabricating evidence against me. Now, Commissioner Otero's brother-in-law makes a case against me. Commissioner Otero vowed revenge on me and has the support of his family for this."

The audience in the courtroom murmurs, and the judge asks for order.

"Mr. Field, don't think this will go unpunished. I will file a complaint and believe this is the end of attorney Francis Ford's career. You should also know that it doesn't exonerate you from county code violations, so I give you a month to correct them."

Nick responds. "That will be impossible, because the same day that lawyer Francis went to take the photos and informed me of the violations, I tried to correct them. All the men that I've tried to hire complain about the amounts of obstacles the city has put in their way, denying them permits and requiring ridiculous blueprints of all kinds as if they were building a skyscraper. In short, it would cost between permit expenses and licenses forty thousand dollars to put a ramp and enlarge two doors. I'm fighting a monster with a lot of power and low morale. I just want to add that I do not give up and that I will expose the corrupt who tries to take the bread off my children's table."

The excited judge stands up and responds. "I congratulate you, Mr. Field, what we are missing is people like you who are not afraid to fight and to stand up to anyone, no matter who it is."

One student screams. "The Viking for President."

The entire audience stands up and applauds even the judge. The judge suddenly realizes that she is part of the circus that she said she would not allow in her room under any circumstances. The judge stops applauding abruptly and sits down.

"Order, order in the room."

Everyone calms down, and the judge tells Nick. "You try to correct those violations, write the name of the people who put those obstacles and let me know. I will make sure that the authorities investigate. You can go now, and I want you to know that I didn't like you, but this has made me reflect and I feel admiration for you. Good luck to you."

The news spread like an uncontrolled fire. Nick made national news again, and the headlines were. The Miami Herald wrote: "THE VIKING DID IT AGAIN." The New York Time wrote: "LAWYER AND WITNESS IN A CASE AGAINST THE VIKING END UP IN JAIL." The Washington

Post wrote: "NICHOLAS FIELD, HATE HIM, LOVE HIM OR FEAR HIM."

CHAPTER FIVE

The interview.

After the last incident in court, Nick felt a relief. The police did not follow him, and the inspectors stopped passing through his business that often. Brandon, Namir, and Victor visited Nick early in the morning.

"Hello, guys. What brings you around here?"

Namir replies. "We come to see how you are doing with the code correction."

Nick scratches his head and responds. "Thanks to the judge's pressure, the city approved the plans and granted the permits. Now I wait for the bank to approve a line of credit so I can pay the contractor. This is ridiculous. It's almost forty thousand dollars."

Brando gives Nick an envelope and says. "Namir is our computer specialist. We opened a website where we explain your situation and open a go fund me account in the bank for those who would like to collaborate. Yesterday, we closed the page because the response was surprising. We receive donations from almost every state in the nation."

Nick is surprised. He doesn't know what to say. Brandon tells him.

"What's the matter, aren't you going to open the envelope?"

Nick takes off his glasses. He is visibly excited.

"Guys, you shouldn't bother; I have no words to thank you for your actions."

Nick opens the envelope and sees a check for thirty-five thousand dollars. Nick hugs each of the students. He couldn't help but let his tears flow from joy. Your actions has shown me that all is not lost, and that my children have a wonderful future with youth like you.

Namir tells Nick. "Based on the surprising response we received to raise these funds, we have realized that your popularity goes beyond our state. We're going to create another website where we'll ask the nation if they would vote for you for the presidency of the country."

Nick laughs and raises his arms. "No, no, no, you have gone crazy. I am just a clown who has fallen into grace because of incidents that the press disseminated, but from there to president there is an enormous gap."

Brandon replies. "The people will decide that, and I believe that all those people who contributed to your cause believe in you and your qualities. Please don't let us down."

Nick feels committed not only to the students but to the thousands of donors who had selflessly supported him at a critical time.

"Okay, but what do you guys have in mind."

Victor responds. "We have contacted the producer of the program America Decides. We asked him to interview you. He told us you are a charismatic and popular person, but you are not a politician, nor have you presented any intention of being a politician. When I told him about our idea, he laughed and replied that if you get four million votes, you could count on the interview."

Nick puts both hands-on Victor's shoulders and mockingly responds. "Then there's no problem, but then don't feel bad when the results differ from what you are expecting. No one is going to take a mechanic with no political experience seriously."

Nick goes out to say goodbye to the students and sees that they don't have the Viking helmet on the roof of the Volkswagen. "What happened to the helmet?"

The students laugh and Brandon responds. "We didn't put it on because we were afraid you would refuse, but since you gave us the green light, today your campaign begins."

The students take the large Viking helmet out of the back seat and put it on the roof of the Volkswagen, then put magnetic signs on the doors that read "Nick Field, my president."

The students leave and Nick looks at Mark, who was jumping and shouting, "The Viking for President." Roberto laughed out loud and shouted, "The Viking, the Viking!" Nick yells at them. "Shut the hell up and get to work."

Nick waited for dinner time to reveal the news. Brittany, Nick's wife, tells him. "I see you differently today. You are more happy than usual. What's going on Nick?"

Nick's son was a twelve-year-old boy who physically resembles his father and, adding to the curiosity of his mother, asks. "Dad, did you win the lottery?"

Nick runs his hand over his son's head and responds. "No Tommy, but something like that."

Nick's daughter was a beautiful ten-year-old girl named Kathy, with curiosity, she says. "If you earned something, remember that you promised me to buy me a computer."

Brittany stops serving the soup and threatens Nick with the scoop. "You talk or I hit your head with the scoop."

Kathy raises her hand and says. "No mom, if you hit him, he won't buy me the computer."

Nick puts the envelope with the check on the table and says. "You guys will not believe this."

Brittany takes the envelope and responds. "What is this, another subpoena for the court?"

Nick doesn't answer, and Brittany opens the envelope. Brittany covers her mouth with her hand and exclaims. "My God! Where did this come from? "

Nick tells his wife what happened during the morning at the shop. Brittany did not come out of her amazement; her eyes were watered with emotion. Brittany hugs her husband and tells him. "Finally, good news. It was about time for us to receive something nice. What I don't understand is how you accepted the student's proposal, knowing that with your luck, everything is possible."

Nick looks at her seriously and replies. "You are not serious? I understand those kids who are inexperienced young people full of energy and illusions, but you well know that the reality is quite different. That's the major leagues, where you need a lot of sponsors and a lot of money. Everyone who comes to that position is because they have committed to someone. Big companies invest millions of dollars to secure their interests. Nobody would allow a nobody to take such a position so their profits would be threatened," Nick replied seriously.

Brittany moves her head from side to side and responds. "I agree with you, but you gave your word to those young kids. What would happen if you get to four million votes?"

Nick laughs out loud. "But you also got infected with those guys?"

"Seriously Nick What would you do then?"

Nick stops laughing and responds. "Then I'll have to give the interview if the producer wants to do it, but I doubt that will happen."

Kathy excitedly asks. Will we go to live in the white house?

Nick kisses her and responds. "Would you like to live in the white house, princess?"

"Yes, dad I would love to."

Nick looks at her, smiles and responds. "Then I promise you that you will live in the white house."

Kathy joyfully closes her fists and raises her arms.

"Yeah! Are you going to be president?"

"No daughter, I'm going to paint our house white."

Brittany, Tommy and Nick laugh. Kathy clutches her eyebrows, crosses her arms and responds. "That's not funny."

Namir immediately set to work on creating the promotion and consultation website for Nick's campaign. The students were very cautious and professional in their creation so that everyone who entered the page would take Nick as a potential candidate. The group of students had grown to twenty, who pledged to campaign thoroughly if Nick got the four million votes in a month.

What would be the surprise for everyone when at the end of the month Nick had received four million five hundred thousand votes. The students held a party at Nick's shop and put-up political banners throughout the business. Nick had no heart to refuse before the students, they had worked hard to achieve such a goal.

Nick was sure that the enthusiasm of the students would soon end, and they would understand that the reality was quite different. The local press was present, but only out of curiosity since there were no other events that made news. Only the Miami Herald reported through mockery: "THE VIKING WANTS TO BE PRESIDENT" and posted a photo of Nick and his family surrounded by the students.

Brandon contacts the producer of the show America Decides and tells him.

"Mr. Steven, Brandon Smith speaking to you, we spoke two months ago. You promised to interview our candidate, Nick Field, if he got to four million votes. Nick passed that amount by half a million votes."

Steven laughs and responds. "Yes, of course I remember. We talked about the Viking. He is a charismatic, controversial, comical character, everything but a politician. I don't think the public will take him seriously and we have a reputation to protect. Airtime is very expensive in a national network, and we have a financial responsibility to our shareholders. If the rating of our programming goes down for a program like that, I would have to answer to my superiors."

Steven thinks that after an explanation like this Brando will give up, but Brandon responds.

"How much does an audience of four and a half million represent in terms of ratings?"

Steven responds. "That's a good rating."

"In that case, consider that if four and a half million took the trouble to vote for that person, they wouldn't be able to sit down and watch his interview. I promise to do a commercial promoting that interview and I assure you that your audience would be at least ten million that day."

Steven laughs and responds. "I must admit that you have a good point in what you say, but first I must investigate whether those votes are correct or are a fraud produced by a computer program."

Brandon responds immediately. "We are the most interested in that those votes being true, so we included on the page the verification system, "I am not a robot," before the person could vote."

Steven responds. "That doesn't matter. We will do an investigation and if our experts testify that there was no manipulation, I will think about doing the interview."

Steven hangs up the phone and Brando screams. "Yes, we will have an interview."

The next day in the afternoon, Brandon, Namir and Victor show up at Nick's business to give him the news of the significant possibility that he would have an interview on the national network. Mark yells at them from inside a car he was fixing. "Long live the Red Beard Viking"

Nick sees the red Volkswagen Beatle in the parking lot with the Viking helmet and Nick Field sign for the president. Nick decides not to leave the office and wait for the students inside the office. As soon as the students enter the office, they look at the wall and notice that Nick has changed the clock elsewhere.

Namir asks. "Why did you change the clock site?"

Nick, downplaying it, says. "It's easier for me to see the time from that place where it is now."

Brandon replies. "The site we chose has its reasons. Everyone who comes in sees it and it serves as a free advertisement. You just have to move your head to your left to see it; I don't think it's a big problem for you."

Nick doesn't willingly respond. "I didn't know you guys were going to tell me how to tidy up my office. I think you're crossing the line."

Namir, for being a woman and more persuasive, responds to him. "We don't want to control you, and we apologize if you've taken us that way. We only want the best for you, and we look at details that, however insignificant they may seem, can make a difference in the end. Please, if it does not bother you, could put it where it was."

Nick doesn't want to argue with the students, and he feels very grateful for everything they've done for him. Nick gets up from his chair and takes the clock and puts it in the place chosen by the students. And asks. "Satisfied?"

Students applaud and shout. "Bravo, now let's take a picture."

After taking the picture with Nick and the clock behind them, Brandon tells him.

"We have good news. The producer of the program America Decide promised us that if he could verify that the four point five million votes were valid, he would grant you an interview. Do you know what that means? You will take your message nationally without interruptions."

Nick puts his hand on his forehead and responds. "You don't stop at anything. I never thought we would get this far. That's why I followed the game. I am not prepared for those things; I am going to make a fool of myself before the nation and you will feel let down because of me."

All three students respond almost unanimously. "No, never. We trust you and we know you speak your truth, that it is our truth. We don't care about the ratings or what they will say, we only care about carrying the message and no one better than you. If we don't win, we will at least plant the seed in someone's consciousness who in the future might bring changes. You don't owe that to us, but to your children."

Nick was moved by Brando's words. He gave each of them a firm handshake and responded. "You're right. I owe it to you and to my children. I'm going to do the interview."

It had been exactly one month since Brandon had spoken to Steven. Brandon for two weeks impatiently waited for Steve's call, when his phone rings.

"Hi Brandon, is Steven. How are you doing?"

Brandon almost screamed with joy but held back. "Well, thank you, and now much better with your call."

Steven replies. "I must tell you that my team was impressed with your work. After an exhaustive review, they determined that Nick's votes were legitimate, so I congratulate you. We have scheduled the interview on the fifteenth of next month and it will air two weeks later."

Brandon almost speechlessly responds. "Perfect, we will send you our commercial."

"No thanks, Brandon, that would promote Nick and our show is called America Decide. We announce the topics to be discussed on Mondays and Wednesdays to promote our program. There are four topics of fifteen minutes each minus the five of commercials that Nick will be on camera for about ten minutes, where he must answer five questions with a time of two minutes for answers. "

Brandon responds. "Excellent. What are the questions?"

"I'm sorry Brandon, but we don't tell anyone what we're going to ask so they can respond spontaneously and show the mastery they have over the situation or the issue to be addressed. Remember that it is America decides."

"You are absolutely right, and I think it's the right thing to do. Where will the interview be?"

Steven replies. "Our cameras will interview him in his shop. America needs to know who he is, what he does and how he lives. If you can read between the lines, I gave you a good idea about what we will ask. Will you be present that day?"

Brando responds. "No, and only Nick will know. I want you to report the truth of who he is, what he does and how he lives without altering reality."

"I like that, and I see it as very positive." Steven replies.

The next day, Brandon shows up at Nick's shop and finds him working on a car. "Nick, can you give me just five minutes in your office?"

Nick takes a deep breath and responds. "Brandon, I like you a lot, but I have to work to pay my bills. I don't want to be rude to you. Understand me and don't get angry."

Brandon replies. "I understand you perfectly. It will be only five minutes."

Nick puts down his tools and heads to the office. Mark and Roberto follow him with their eyes as if trying to decipher what was happening. Once in the office, Brandon tells him.

"They will interview you on the fifteenth of next month, right here in your workshop for the America Decide program. Don't tell anyone so that everything is natural. We want the public to see that you are an ordinary person."

Nick puts his hands on his head. "You will not stop until I become a real president."

Brandon responds. "We just want the best for the country. I want you to prepare to answer three questions."

Nick moves his head negatively. "You're wrong Brandon, I don't have to prepare for anything. That is conditioning my convictions. I will respond as I see things. If that doesn't suit you, then cancel the interview."

Brando was speechless. The Viking was a person of powerful character and firm convictions. It would not be easy to run a campaign that way. The only thing that motivated him to move on was that they both shared the same values.

"It will be as you say Nick, I just want you to look good on camera."

Nick replies again with the same rudeness. "I don't care if I don't look good in front of the cameras; I'd rather give a poor impression than a fake one. You should know me a little better if you want to campaign with me."

It convinced Brandon that it would not be a simple task for them.

"Okay Nick, I just want to ask you one last thing on behalf of all of us."

Nick reluctantly responds. "I have to work. You told me five minutes. What else do you want now?"

"We bought you that wall clock and asked you to allow us to choose the place to put it. You agreed, but you've moved it twice. If you don't want to put it where we asked for it, then don't accept it and we'll take it away."

Nick is totally angry and picks up the clock and gives it to Brandon. "Look, Brando, take the fucking clock and put it wherever that hell you want, if it is so important to you. I will not change it, or if you want, take it with you, but I have to work. Nobody pays my bills."

Nick steps out of the office and leaves Brandon in the office with the clock in his hand. Brandon thinks for a few moments. He thinks it would be best to finish it all right there, but puts the clock back in the chosen place and waits for the results of the interview.

Nick didn't tell anyone about the interview and went on with his normal life. The students didn't contact him anymore and Nick felt bad, knowing he hadn't been polite at all with Brandon on his last visit. Nick calls Brandon to apologize and Brandon replies.

"I'm in classes. I can't talk to you now. Some people work and others study. I call you after class."

Nick looked at his cell phone, opened his eyes in surprise, and he put it in his pocket. About two hours later, Nick gets a call from Brandon.

"Hi Nick, sorry that I could not talk to you. I was in classes. Tell me what you need?"

Nick responds. "I need to apologize; I don't think I was very kind to you last time, and you didn't deserve the way I treated you."

"You don't have to worry, I just want you to understand that, if you're going to be a political figure, that means you have to be more cautious with your words, you can't always treat people that way because, even if your intentions are good, they will call you a dictator. Words are like bullets. After they come out, you can never take them back. You will be the master of what you what you don't say and a slave to what you do say."

Nick was impressed with Brandon's words; he didn't expect so much wisdom from a young man. Brandon had given him a lesson.

"Excuse Me Brandon, I'm not used to these things, but you're absolutely right and I think you don't have to be a politician to watch what you say. More than an apology, I thank you for making me reflect."

Brandon responds. "You don't know the joy it gives me to hear that from you. And the clock. Did you change its place?"

"I gave you my word. It will be on that wall until you decide otherwise."

The day of the interview arrived, and Nick thought they had canceled it, because it was almost time to close, and no one has shown up. Suddenly Nick sees a white van parked in his parking lot, then sees a cameraman and the famous host of the program America Decide, Mr. Steven Wright. Nick was all dirty and full of motor oil because, seeing that it was 11:00 AM and no one had arrived, he went to work as usual.

Steven turns to Nick and asks. Where do you want to do the interview?

Nick responds. "This is a small, humble place. It won't change at all where we do it."

Steven responds. "I like your answer. Let's do it here, you and I standing, and your two employees are visible behind us."

The cameraman prepares his camera and says. "We start in one, two and three."

"Nicholas Field, the Viking, as many, know him, but who is the Viking?"

Nick looks directly at the camera and responds.

"I am the Viking, you are the Viking, that camera man who is recording this interview is the Viking, that person watching this interview is the Viking and those people who are working to feed their family and cannot see this interview are also Vikings, because it is not me only the Viking, the country is full of Vikings who fight for a better tomorrow for their family."

Steven asks. " What does Nicholas Field do?"

Nick turns around and shows the shop and responds. For fifteen years, I dedicated myself to this. Many people think that because I am the owner, I have privileges or that I am an exploiter. But I cannot take a vacation like those who work for a large company or the government.

I answer for the salary of those two workers, who more than workers are my family. They go before me. But I'm not complaining, this business has honestly put bread on the table for my kids and pays the mortgage on my house. Life is full of sacrifices and my parents sacrificed for me without asking for days off. "

Steven questions. "How is a day like in the life of Nicholas Field?"

"It starts very early; we all have breakfast before everyone leave to their job or school. My wife prepares breakfast while I make sure my children are ready for school and check their homework, then I take them to the school bus stop and wait with them until the bus takes them away. After that, I return home and stay with my wife for a while until she goes to work. Then I come to work until 6:00 PM. It's a routine that hasn't changed since we had our first child twelve years ago. But Sundays are sacred, Sundays are for the family."

Steven asks. What motivates you to enter politics?

"I never thought of becoming a politician and I don't consider myself a politician, but I can't tolerate injustices and corruption either. I owe everything to a group of young students from the university who have believed in me and given me their support. As you know, those four and a half million people who basically don't know me and voted for me, did not vote for me, but against those who are in power today. Scandals plagued both the Democratic and Republican conventions from the beginning. We mention that those were their best candidates. I am convinced that whoever wants to be a public servant cannot start by deceiving the public. But if your goal is to enrich yourself from the people, then I can understand that attitude. I am a man of the people, and my primary mission is the prosperity of the people."

Steven asks his last question. Don't you think your message is populist?

"No, I just say what I think. A populist message would be to offer the people benefits to buy their vote, knowing that you will not keep your promises. I am not an enemy of the rich, they are the ones who provide employment and develop the country. That small class that is accused of all evil, just for being rich. They are the backbone of our economy. If we eliminate the rich, we will destroy our economy. The working class is the oxygenated blood that keeps our economy alive and strong. If we neglect that working class, we will make our economy sick and only increase poverty. The ideal is to look for a middle ground where both classes prosper simultaneously with no friction."

Steven turns to the camera and says.

"This concludes our interview with Nicholas Field, the Red-beard Viking, as he is affectionately called in Miami, a controversial figure who ended the career and political aspirations of the two leading candidates for the presidency of the Republican and Democratic parties, then ended the career of a police officer and finally sent the lawyer and the witness who brought charges against him to jail. Nicholas Field showed these individuals were guilty of crimes ranging from fraud to fabricating evidence. Nicholas single-handedly unmasked them and sent them to jail. The Viking knows how to wield his sword. This is it for this week. See you next week on another America Decide show."

CHAPTER SIX

Nick accepts the nomination.

At the headquarters of both parties, they saw Nick as a candidate who could take votes away from their candidate, but not as an adversary who could win the presidency. The new Democratic nominee was California Gov. Charles Hudson, a sixty-two-year-old millionaire who had made his fortune in real estate. Despite being very wealthy, he had not put a penny of his own money for the campaign, but he had raised seventy million dollars so far.

Candidate Charles Hudson meets with his advisers to discuss Nick's interview and they conclude Nick is just a hot-air balloon that will deflate eventually and they should not spend energy on him.

The new candidate of the Republican Party was the senator for the state of South Carolina named Walter Spencer, a seventy-year-old man who has been in politics all his life. During the meeting with his advisors to analyze Nick's interview, they concluded Nick does not represent any danger, that his interview was monotonous and without political content. Walter tells his advisers. Steven's comments about Nick at the end of the interview might help that clown, but he will soon be forgotten as he hasn't started his campaign yet. He has no money or anywhere to get it from. No company will give money to a clown who does not know how to remunerate their donations."

Namir again does another poll on voting intention to see what the public reaction has been after the interview. At the end of the month, Nick reaches twenty-six million votes in the poll. Namir had not informed Nick about the survey. On the day they closed the survey, they decide to give the news to Nick after finishing classes. Students arrive at Nick's shop in Victor's van with the iconic Viking helmet on the roof and see two vans with satellite antennas from two local channels. Namir says angrily. "These guys have been monitoring our survey, and they got ahead of us, breaking the news to Nick."

Nick was in his shop being interviewed by two reporters simultaneously, reporter Rick Rogers from the English-speaking channel and reporter Raul Fernandez from the Spanish-speaking channel. Nick's face was one of pure amazement. Nick did not know that Namir had run a second poll after they aired his interview on national television. Rick Rogers asks.

Did you ever think that you would get twenty million voting intentions?

"I am sorry, but I don't know what you're talking about. I only got four and a half million votes." Nick responds, confused.

Raul Fernandez asks him. "You didn't know of the second popular poll that was done after your interview on the program America Decide?"

Nick opens his eyes and responds. "Wow! That's news to me. I didn't know about that survey."

Roger asks. "Will you campaign full time after these results?"

Nick is thoughtful and sees the students getting out of the van. He responds by pointing at the students.

"Those young people are the reason I've gotten to this point. This has been a chain of events where they have been present all the time, playing the primary role in this. This interview should be with them, not with me."

Reporters waste no time and head towards students. Roger asks. "Who among you is in charge of Nicholas Field's campaign?"

Brandon responds. "We are the original group of fifteen students who saw in Nick the talent, courage and principles needed for a leader. From the first moment, his charisma attracted us. Today after this survey, we are convinced that Nicholas Field, our Viking, is unstoppable and we have faith in his talent, courage, and principles. We want to inform you that our campaign officially begins today. This will be a media campaign because we do not have the millions that the two opposing parties have. I am the campaign manager; Namir is our head of promotion and Victor oversees finance. Everyone else is as important as we are, because we depend on each other."

Reporter Raul turns to Victor and asks. "How much money do you have raised for the campaign?"

Victor responds. "As Brandon just told you, we just started our campaign, but let's see, guys."

Victor puts his hand out for money. Each of the students put in twenty dollars. Mark runs and puts in twenty dollars and Roberto gives a fifty-dollar bill. Victor returns the fifty-dollar bill to Roberto and tells him.

"I'm so sorry Grandpa, but the maximum contribution we accept is twenty dollars."

Roberto changes his fifty for a twenty and Victor says, "We just started, and we have already collected one hundred dollars."

Everyone laughs, and reporter Raul asks. "Why a maximum of twenty dollars?"

Brandon responds. "Because when a politician receives millions in donations, he is in debt with the donors Those millions allow the donor to have a significant influence on the politician's decisions, but in our case, we believe that twenty dollars cannot give much power to the donor."

Everyone laughs again, and Roger tells them. "Very well thought out. I agree with you."

Reporter Raul takes twenty dollars out of his wallet and gives it to Victor. "Here is my contribution."

After the reporters leave, the students, Nick, Mark and Roberto, gather in the office to celebrate. The students had brought two bottles of champagne to celebrate. Nick hadn't spoken out on the subject; everything had been so sudden that he didn't know what to do or say. Roberto asks for the floor and says. "Guys, all this has been very nice. But now, what's next?"

Nick says. "Guys, I am very proud of you, but before I solve the problems of the world, I have to solve mine. I have to work to feed my family. I can't dedicate myself to traveling to campaign and stop paying my bills."

Namir responds. "We know, and that's why we have a strategy that's going to take them all by surprise. You will continue working in your shop and we will take care of everything. We will monitor the campaigns of the opposing parties and you will send a message to the people from your shop weekly. You will officially enter the electoral contest as late as the law allows. The federal government, by law, has funds available for independent candidates, plus any money that we will raise will cover your expenses. At some point, you must leave the shop to prepare and take part in the national debates."

Nick finally speaks and says. "I must talk to my family. I need to think about it. In three days, I will give my answer."

Brandon replies. "Nick, I just want you to remember that your commitment is not just to us fifteen. There are twenty-six million people who gave their vote of confidence in you, and you also owe it to your children. If you change your mind, don't complain if those who represent you let you down once again."

Nick stays thoughtful and says again. "I will give you my answer in three days. Take a three days' vacation, because if I decide to do it, we will not have no time to rest for a long time."

That night during dinner, Nick tells his wife what happened in the workshop. Brittany was unaware that her husband had received twenty-six million voting intentions. Brittany tells her husband.

"I will support whatever decision you make, but I don't want you to do it out of commitment to anyone. As far as I'm concerned, the only thing I care about is our family. I am not afraid of the press. I have nothing to hide but remember, if the press has besieged us being no one, I do not want to think how it will be if you decide to run."

The conversation is interrupted when on the news they are interviewing the Republican candidate, Walter Spencer, and asking him. "Do you care about the twenty-six million vote intentions that Nicholas Field got in the last poll?"

Walter responds. "Yes, I worry a lot, but not because I consider him a serious candidate or with possibilities. I worry that the electoral process is losing its seriousness and that people with ambition of camera and popularity will use the electoral process to satiate their narcissism. Those twenty-six million don't take Mr. Field seriously. They just have fun and should pay more attention to the problems this Democratic administration has caused rather than following the Viking circus, as they call it. Just the nickname of the Red-beard Viking takes away the seriousness of the process."

A flushed Nick looks at his wife, who sees the Nick did not like Walter's comment at all. Then they introduce

Democratic hopeful Charles Hudson and basically ask him the same question. Charles responds emphatically and belittling Nick.

"I'm not worried at all; our voters know all too well the difference between running a mechanic shop and running the most powerful country in the world."

Those were the words that ended up convincing Nick. Brittany looks at him and sees that Nick is furious because they have ridiculed him before the nation. Brittany says to him in a soft, but firm voice. "I know what you're thinking, and I'm ready to go all the way with you. That disrespect was against all of us, not just against you."

Nick stands up, picks up the phone, and calls Brandon. "Hello Brando, forgive me for bothering you, but I don't need three days. My answer is yes, you can count on me."

Brandon laughs and replies. "You also just watched the national news?"

"Yes, I just saw it." Nick replies.

"They are so arrogant that they are destroying themselves and they don't know it. Tomorrow, I will tell Namir to open an account for you on Facebook, Twitter, and Instagram. We will not respond to them immediately; we will only take notes to give a weekly response. Victor's uncle will lend us a place where we will have our headquarters. We will condition it tomorrow."

Nick asks. "What do you want me to do?"

"You just enjoy your family; difficult and hectic days are coming. Try to update yourself as much as possible in international politics for future debates. You must polish yourself while still being who you are because that's what the people want. The people are tired of politicians and politicking. The people want that Viking who shoots straight and fight to defend their interest."

Brandon, Namir and Victor get to work on the campaign. Brandon contacts English-language channel reporter Rick Rogers to inform him they will start Nick's campaign. Brandon tried to reach reporter Raul Fernandez from the Hispanic channel and found out that Fernandez was fired for donating twenty dollars to Nick's campaign on camera. The channel gave a statement saying Raul crossed the line between journalism and activism. Brandon seized the moment and Fernandez's popularity in the Hispanic community to hire him as the campaign spokesperson.

Local news reported the beginning of Nick's campaign, but not with much enthusiasm or seriousness in the news since Nick would not pay for political commercials or promise concessions to anyone. The official candidates opted for ignoring Nick because if they talked about him, it will be like recognize him as an opponent.

Namir set up a platform where voters could ask questions and Nick daily answered three questions to stay in touch with the people. In addition, once a week, Nick sent a two-minute message to the nation. Nick not only kept his supporters, but gradually gained more support. Brandon's strategy was working and worrying the opposition parties Every day while Nick was working in the shop, Brandon would approach him and ask him questions taken from the emails received. They recorded this on Mark's cell phone and then uploaded to the social media.

Brandon approaches Nick while he was doing an oil change on a vehicle and asks him. "A twenty-year-old boy from Colorado named Frank Watson asks if you would do mandatory military service. "

Nick turns around and responds.

"I would not impose mandatory service unless it is a national emergency. That would be like paying for a university degree for someone who doesn't want to study. It is far better to use those funds to give better conditions and armaments to those who voluntarily decide to enter the armed forces. Those who with no pressure enlist to defend our nation and the freedom we enjoy deserve a better retirement and student help. A Vietnam veteran will receive more aid if he enters illegally through the Mexican border than what his government gives him. "

Nick's weekly comments and the answers to the questions eroded the campaign of the major parties. The polls did not mention Nick and only gave results from the Republican and Democratic candidates. The acquisition of the reporter Raul Fernandez paid off when, through his contacts, he entered a radio interview with California Governor Charles Hudson. Raul asks. "Why don't you include Nicholas Field when you do the polls?"

The governor was upset with the question and answers. "First. I am not the one making the polls. Second, he is not included because he is not a serious candidate. He hasn't been registered himself in any state. He just wants popularity and camera. "

Raul replies. "Nick has been very clear that he will register himself seven months before the election. Any independent candidate can register late without penalty. They must only meet the requirements that the state asks of them. But that doesn't mean he hasn't been in contact with the people, it is that just he doesn't have the funds."

Charles hangs up the call abruptly and takes advantage of it being a radio program and that the audience can see it. "Only a coward or a person without an argument speaks and then hangs up. But you will not get away with it, my friend, because I will answer you, so that the thousands of radio listeners will see that I face any question regardless of what the question might be."

The next day, in the weekly commentary, Nick speaks from his office.

"Good afternoon, dear citizens. You know that I have a magnetism to unmask false politicians and this time will be no different. Yesterday, our campaign spokesperson, Raul Fernandez, entered the radio program where California Governor Charles Hudson was interviewed. Governor Charles was upset with Raul's comments and, having no response, simply hung up the call and then accused him of being a coward. What Governor Charles didn't know was that the call was recorded on the campaign manager's phone and was out loud. You can see in the video that we will put on the air that at no time Raul hangs up the call and you can also hear Charles' comments because the radio is heard simultaneously. Charles took advantage of the audience, who couldn't see what happened. You watch the video and draw your own conclusions about who is the coward here."

Nick points to the office TV and broadcasts the video of the radio interview where Raul was talking to Governor Charles. Nick made national news again by unmasking Governor Charles Hudson. To remedy the damage, Charles meets the announcer at a restaurant.

Charles tells the announcer Daniel Vertuchi. "Daniel, I need your help. Only you can get me out of this mess. I will be eternally indebted to you."

Daniel knew Charles personally and had not commented on the incident because he knew Charles would have to come to him for help. Daniel puts on a worried face and asks Charles. "What do you want me to do?"

Charles responds. "You are the only person who can make this go away. If you say that without realizing it and by mistake you pressed the button that hung up the call. You can say that you never intended to create such a problem that you accept responsibility for what happened. Just tell that you didn't say anything because you didn't think this was going to take on dimensions beyond what it warrants."

Daniel looks at Charles and smiles. "This makes me look terrible and you know it."

"Yes, I know, but tell me how can I make it up to you?"

Daniel takes a deep breath, stays thoughtful, and then responds.

"I will do it for my son. He is going to enter the Los Angeles University and he will need a place to live. Maybe you can help him with one of the many houses you have in the area."

Charles understood Daniel was charging him the dear favor, but he had no choice. "Consider it done. I will have an apartment near the university; I will cover all the expenses."

Daniel responds. "No, that's not a good idea. My son is not used to living in apartments. He has always lived at home where he can play his music or meet with his friends without disturbing the neighbors. I wouldn't want the neighbors to give complaints, which would ultimately connect him to you and this incident."

Charles understood that he would have to pay a high price for the favor. "I understand. I'll get you a house as close as I can to college."

Daniel responds. "I remember that it's five years of college and then he would like to stay in Los Angeles because he is studying sound engineering and wants to work for a film company. A young boy cannot afford such exorbitant expenses."

Charles reddened and furious replies. "Do you want me to give a house to your son? In that area, houses cost at least a million and a half in exchange for your favor?"

Daniel's undeterred responds. "You want me to ruin my career by taking responsibility for what you did? A million and a half is not much for you. You just think about how much you have invested in your presidential career."

Charles loses control and slaps the table. "I thought you had a little more principles and valued my friendship. I see you want to take advantage of my situation to make yourself a million and a half."

Daniel, without losing control, gently responds. "You are no friend of anyone, and you have no right to talk about principles. I have told you how much it will cost after you asked me to do something dishonest to save your skin. You take it or leave it, but if you leave it, I warn you I have to answer the listeners this Monday and questions related to that incident are inevitable. If I do not receive ownership of that house by Monday, my answers will be truthful and forceful. Finally, the next time you invite an Italian to a restaurant, make sure it's to a real Italian restaurant. This spaghetti tastes like shit."

Daniel stands up and leaves without saying goodbye to Charles, who follows him with his eyes until Daniel exits the restaurant.

On Monday, about fifteen minutes before Daniel Vertucci's show aired, Daniel receives a package which Charles Hudson had sent him with great urgency. Daniel opens the package and sees that it is the title of a house. Daniel wastes no time and quickly enters the internet. Google the address of the house and sees that it is a four-bedroom, two-bathroom house near the university valued at a million three hundred thousand dollars. Daniel smiles maliciously and closes the computer.

Daniel begins his radio show by saying.

"Good afternoon, dear radio listeners. I know everyone is eager to hear my version of what happened during the interview with Governor Charles Hudson. I am sure you have lots of questions about it, so I will start by saying that all this has been a chain of misunderstandings and I am the one to blame. I only understood what had happened when a friend this morning sent me the video of Nicholas Field accusing Governor Charles of hanging up the call to his campaign spokesperson Raúl Fernández and then insulting him. Both Nicholas and Charles are wrong because it was me who inadvertently hung up the call and then thought that Raul had hung up the call based on Charles' comments. I apologize to you, Mr. Raul Fernandez and Governor Charles Hudson.

I want to clarify that at no time I intended to favor Governor Charles or harm Mr. Fernandez or Nicholas Field. I reached out to Governor Charles this morning and explained what had actually happened during the interview. He has expressed to his deep regret for the words he uses in his comment about Mr. Fernandez because he expressed himself based on what he thought had happened. Once again, I apologize to all those affected by my mistake and hope you understand I am a human being; I also make mistakes."

With such a comment, Daniel Vertuchi ripped a million three hundred thousand dollars from Charles Hudson and remained before the public as an individual who is not afraid to recognize his mistakes and great moral integrity. But that comment repaired Nick's damage to Charles' campaign.

Namir was recruiting students at every university in the nation through her website and the campaign was taking shape and strength day by day. That was noticed by both parties who separately sabotaged Nick's campaign. Victor receives a call informing him that his uncle's place where they had Nick's campaign headquarters had caught fire. The place was destroyed. What it did not burn in the fire was damaged by the excessive amount of water used by the firefighters.

The students gathered in front of the premises, and the press interviewed them. Nick appears on the scene; it was the first time Nick left his job to go to something related to his campaign. It shocked Nick to see the students crying helplessly. The cameras quickly turn to Nick, who does not hesitate for a moment to express his doubts about the incident.

"When these young people put the headquarters in this place, all kinds of inspectors rained on us, both from the county and the city. These were the most extensive and exhaustive inspection I've ever seen. Three months later, the place catches fire because of a short circuit. I think those wires instead of being made of copper, they were made of gasoline to create such a fire and the destruction is total because of the amount of water used to put out the fire. Curiously, the fire station is less than two miles from this place, but it took fifteen minutes for the fire units to arrive. All this is more than rare, but now more than ever, we will move forward. This just shows that we are moving forward."

The fire chief was at the scene, and upon hearing Nick's comments, intervened.

"Are you accusing the fire department of being involved in a criminal act?"

Nick responds right away. "I have no evidence to accuse the department of having committed a criminal act, but at least to declare them incompetent and negligent. Can you justify a fifteen-minute response when you are within two miles of the fire?"

The fire chief was speechless. His face showed frustration and bewilderment. The reporter puts the microphone to the chief. The reporter, seeing that the chief was not responding, tells him. "Do you have an answer to justify the delay of your department?"

"I will not comment without investigating the incident."

The chief turns around and runs away from the scene. It was almost impossible to determine who was responsible for the fire at Nick's campaign headquarters, as Nick had enemies in the city, in the county, in the state and now national wide.

CHAPTER SEVEN

Nick is accused of rape.

The burning of Nick's campaign headquarters won him great sympathy nationwide, and Namir seized the moment to accept donations. The response was surprising. In just three days, they raised fifty thousand dollars. Namir not only put the money raised on the website, but also detailed how they spent the money. That financial transparency had great acceptance in the public and increased donations.

The Democratic and Republican Parties included Nick in the polls for the first time because of public pressure. The Democratic Party had five candidates and the Republican Party had eight candidates, plus one candidate for the Green Party. Every national television and newspaper in the nation released the poll results with the news on the front page that Nick was in third place behind California Governor Charles Hudson and South Carolina Senator Walter Spencer.

Alarm went off at both campaign headquarters. Governor Charles meets with his team and says, "The burning of the Viking campaign headquarters was a huge mistake. That has only put him where he is now. I would like to know who the stupid idiot was who set it on fire."

Peter Brown was Charles' campaign manager; he responds. "We're not involved in that, but the Viking has so many enemies that it's impossible to know. We can't let him go up in the polls. We need to give him a blow from which he can't recover."

Charles replies. "We all have skeletons hidden in the closet. Look for it and expose it. That will end the Viking's charm."

Peter moves his head and responds. "I've been investigating for months, and we haven't found anything. Either he has no skeletons, or he has no closet, but the stupid jerk is more methodical than a monk. All the scandals in which he has been involved have only catapulted him into the campaign."

Charles punches the table. "Well, then you make a closet and put a skeleton in it and don't involve me in anything. The last time I had a stumble with that riffraff, it cost a lot of money."

Meanwhile, at the Republican campaign headquarters, things were no different. Senator Walter Spencer and his cabinet were discussing strategies to remove Nick from the campaign. Walter asks his campaign manager. "Ronald, what can we do to eliminate that clown who is stealing the show?"

Ronald responds. "Senator, this is a delicate issue. The people see him as a Messiah. I don't know what the fuck that stupid guy has, but everything goes well for him. Student support has branched out through all the universities in the country and has become more of a youth challenge to the traditional political class."

Walter applauds and responds sarcastically. "How nice! I pay you to glorify that asshole. I need results. That idiot has never got out of Florida, has never taken part in the political arena and is in third place ahead of nine established politicians between Republicans and Democrats. I want you, without involving me or the party, to get rid of that man. You are unleashed and have an open checkbook."

Nick sees a car arrive at his workshop with dark windows, like those used by undercover detectives. Nick shakes his head and says to Roberto. "I knew that peace had lasted too long in this place."

Nick sees former Sergeant Stanley get out of the car. Nick, surprised, tells him. "I thought you had retired from the police."

Stanley shakes hands with Nick and responds. "It's true, I retired and was planning to become a private investigator, that's why I bought this vehicle. I learned of the burning of your headquarters."

Nick moves his head and responds. "Those bastards have no limits. We are trying to reopen it, but the inspectors are crucifying us."

Stanley puts his right hand on Nick's shoulder and tells her.

"Nick, wake up. You're playing in the major leagues now. You need someone in charge of your personal safety and the security of your headquarters. None of those students have the ability or experience needed for that job."

Nick shrugs his shoulders and responds. "What am I going to do? That's what I have. I don't have the money to pay someone to do that job."

Stanley laughs and tells him. "The first time I saw you, I felt like tearing your neck off, but that same night, you became my hero. Thanks to your follies, I retired from the police force as a captain. I owe that to you. I have a place that is prepared with the entire system of security cameras so that something like that does not happen again. It's twice as big as the one you had; I want you to move your headquarters to my place."

Nick responds. "Thank you, Stanley, but the place we had was Victor's uncle. He didn't charge us rent; we can't pay for your place."

Stanley responds. "That place is mine. No one has talked about rent. And from now on, I will be your security chief. You don't have to pay me a penny. Just by being the head of security of a presidential candidate, it will bring a lot of customers later. I only ask that when you officially register for the presidential campaign and the feds come to provide you with protection, you keep me on your team. "

Nick had eyes watered with emotion. One of the biggest problems of his campaign had been solved and without incurring expenses. Nick gives Stanley a big hug and says. "You can't imagine the problem you've solved for us. Welcome to our family. Please contact Brandon and let him know the news and don't be angry if those guys carry you as they did with me that night."

Nick's campaign came back to life with Stanley's addition to Nick's group. Now they had a spokesperson who was a professional and a security chief with the experience and contacts. Namir's work on the social media was flawless. They already had students representing the Viking's campaign, as they affectionately called it, in all fifty states of the nation, including Puerto Rico. Nick kept answering three questions a day and kept addressing to the country once a week.

One evening Nick leaves a little later than usual from work and while he stops in a red light, a beautiful young woman of about twenty - three years of age, white complexion, blond hair, blue eyes and an exquisite figure approaches him. She was not the typical resident of the area, which was overwhelmingly Latino. The young woman beckons Nick to roll down his window. Nick rolls down the window and the young woman says.

"If you want to have a good time, I assure you that you will not regret it."

Nick asks. "How much do you charge for a good time?"

"A hundred dollars, but if you don't have a hundred, we can come to an arrangement."

Nick takes out a hundred-dollar bill and gives it to her and tells her. "Go home. You don't have to sell your body. You are young and you are healthy. I am sure you can get ahead in life if you put your mind to it."

The young woman replies. "Thank you. You are an angel. I am living in a motel six blocks from here. Can you give me a ride home?"

Nick knows his car has cameras and that he can prove his innocence if the young woman is setting a trap for him. "If it's in a straight line, I'll take you."

The young woman says. "Yes, it's, just six blocks straight. I thank you sincerely."

The young woman gets into Nick's car and tells him. "Thank you. I didn't think there were people like you."

Nick replies. "You remind me of my younger sister. I would never pay to have sex. I don't judge you or approve of what you do, but I advise you to try other means of making a living. If you live in a motel, that means you're not from here."

The young woman with tears in her eyes responds. "I'm from Oklahoma. I left home because my stepfather abused me since I was nine years old. I told my mother, but she said that I was a liar and an ungrateful evil. I have lived an ordeal for many years, so when I gathered a little money, I left home. I always liked Florida and its beaches, but Miami differs from what I imagine."

Nick moved replies. "I am very sorry for what has happened to you, and I applaud you that have made your way in life, but I advise you to look for another job."

The young woman responds in sorrow. "That's what I try, but if you don't speak Spanish; it's impossible for me to find work here."

Nick laughs and replies. "You are right. What were you working on?"

"I worked in a doctors' office collecting medical bills and filing patient records. I swear to you that if I get a job; I would never work on the street again. Do you think you could help me?"

Nick remains thoughtful and responds. "I have a small mechanical shop and the work has multiplied lately, before I used to leave at 6:30 PM, but now I am leaving later because I have to do all the work in the office. I could hire you if you are interested. I only can pay you eight dollars an hour and you must be punctual."

The young woman gives a shout of joy, gives Nick a kiss on the cheek, and responds.

"Thank you, my angel. I knew God would not abandon me. I promise you that you will not regret it. Give me the address and the schedule that I will be there like a soldier in his post."

Nick parks his vehicle, gives her his business card and tells her. "Here you have all the information you need. It's near to your motel. What's your name?"

The young woman responds. "My name is Cristina. What is your name?"

"My name is Nicholas Field. Have a good night."

The young woman puts the hundred-dollar back on the dashboard of and says.

"I can't accept your money; I'd rather earn it with my work."

Nick replies. "If you need it, take it as an advance on your salary."

Cristina takes the money and responds. "Only then will I take it because I really need it. Thank you, my guardian angel. I see tomorrow."

Upon arriving home, Nick tells his wife Brittany about his encounter with Cristina. Brittany replies, "You have to be careful. Maybe it's a trap."

"I thought that at first, but I think it's true what she told me. I had no heart to leave such a young woman helpless."

Brittany thinks a little and responds. "You always do the right thing, but not everyone acts the same. We'll see how she behaves, but don't let your guard down."

Nick kisses her on the forehead and responds, "I promise you, I will be on the lookout for any strange attitude."

The next day, Nick arrives at the shop and finds Cristina waiting at the entrance.

"Good morning, Cristina. I didn't expect to see you so early."

"I never missed a day or been late in my job. I told you that you will not regret giving me a chance."

Nick opens the shop and explains the work to Cristina. The two are confined to work when Mark comes in and sees Cristina. Mark felt a direct crush on the heart.

"My God, Nick, you always talked about your sister, but you never told us you would bring her to work with you."

"It's not my sister Mark. She is a Cristina, and she will work here in the office. She will help us with the paper's work."

Mark asks Cristina in terrible Spanish. "Do you speak Spanish?"

Cristina laughing responds in her terrible Spanish. "My talk a little."

When Nick leaves the office and enters the shop, Mark tells him.

"Shit Nick: MY TALK ONE LITTLE BIT. But with those tits who need to speak Spanish."

Roberto just listened and laughed mischievously. Nick replies. "Mark, please behave. I met her yesterday and we don't know her that well to be using those jokes."

Mark puts his hand on his head and responds. "You met her yesterday and you already have her here. Your wife is going to catch you, but I understand you because I will marry her tomorrow if she wants."

Roberto can't stand the laughter and Mark tells him. "Laugh. When this spreads in the neighborhood, the shop will be filled with old folks like you trying to look at that ass."

Roberto instantly gets serious and responds. "Listen boy, don't go overboard because you are the only one who doesn't have a woman."

Nick interrupts and scolds them. "Hey! I hired her because that way, we can work the three of us in the shop without having to waste time in the office, so stop fucking around and get to work."

Mark responds. "Are you sure that's just why you hired her?

Roberto laughs again. "Enough, I don't want any more comments."

When Stanley learned of Cristina's presence, he immediately contacted Nick.

"Hi Nick, Brandon informed me you have a young woman working in the shop. You never informed me. What do you know about her?"

"Very little." Nick replies. "If what she says is true, she's from Oklahoma. Her name is Cristina, and she used to work as an office clerk."

"That's all you know about her?"

Nick reluctantly responds. "I didn't know I should inform you of the decisions I make in my business. You're taking your job beyond the limits."

"You are wrong. You do not quite understand that you stopped being an ordinary citizen. You are a public figure and with powerful enemies. You do not know how those people act. Taking precautions is absolutely necessary, and that's what I'm here for."

Nick takes a deep breath and responds. "I will send you a text with her name, address and social security number for you to investigate, and now excuse me, but I have to go to work."

Nick hangs up the phone and says. "This is the only thing I need now; I have to ask permission even to go to the bathroom."

The days went by, and Cristina settled into work and turned out to be a help to Nick. Mark tried to conquer Cristina, but she cordially rejected him. One Friday at the end of the workday, Mark approaches Cristina and tells her.

"How about if we go out tonight? I know a place that I am sure you will love it."

Cristina looks at him and tells him, "Mark, I think I've been very clear to you I'm not interested in having relationships with anyone. Just because I treat you politely doesn't mean I'm giving you any kind of hope. I don't want you to damage our friendship or to feel harass at work."

Nick instantly calls Mark out of the office and tells him. "I think Cristina has been very clear to you, so I ask you to please hold back. I don't need an accusation of sexual harassment in my shop. You know it would hurt me a lot, even if I had no involvement."

Nick turns around and sees that Cristina was behind him with some papers for him to sign and had heard everything. Cristina tells him.

"You're wrong Nick. I am a grateful person, and I would never bite the hand that fed me when I needed it the most. You to me, are like the big brother I never had and always dreamed to have. I would do nothing that would hurt you, but I would like Mark to treat me like a co-worker and nothing else."

Mark embarrassedly apologizes and leaves. Nick thanks Cristina for her understanding and apologizes on behalf of Mark. Cristina gives him the papers and responds. "Just sign these papers for me and let's not talk about it anymore."

Seven months before the presidential election, they officially registered Nick as a candidate for the presidency of the United States. All the media echoed the news as many people thought Nick would not enter the campaign and, as a result, he had fallen from third to sixth place. Nick's entry into the race gave him the needed boost. Nick regained his third place just by making official his candidacy. Donations doubled and financially, they could open headquarters in several states, but they maintained the same campaign style by directly answering three questions a day from the shop and one message to the nation per week.

While Nick was in sixth place, Charles and Walter engaged in a fierce fight between the two, which favored Nick's campaign once he officially enters. The big surprise was when the polls gave a virtual tie between Walter, Charles and Nick. The press kept commenting on the Viking phenomenon. Both parties heard the alarm. It was necessary to slow down the Viking.

Gov. Charles Hudson meets with his team and tells his campaign manager. "Peter, you have not got Nicholas Field out of the way and you haven't done anything."

Peter disgusted replies. "Yes, I put in place a plan to end it once and for all. They are waiting for my order; I have not executed it because he posed no danger. Every time someone tries to attack the fucking Viking, things go the other way; I haven't wanted to take unnecessary risks.

Remember what happened to you in the interview and how much it cost you to amend that mistake."

Charles raises his eyebrows and responds. "Well, give the order and finish the fucking Viking once and for all."

Peter says. "Very good, then I will say to..."

Charles puts both of his hands on a stop sign. "No, no, no. I don't want to know anything about it. "

Peter smiles and responds. "You don't have to worry. My plan leaves no trail. No one can connect us with it."

Charles moves his head and responds. "Very good, Peter, but anyway, I don't want to know. Thank you."

At the headquarters of the Republican Party, the situation was almost identical. Senator Walter Spencer was furious. He could not believe that the points he had gained after Charle's radio interview fiasco had vanished, and now he had to add Nick's entry into the campaign. The virtual tie with Walter and Nick put him at a total disadvantage with only seven months left.

Walter points his finger at his campaign manager and scolds him.

"Ronald, I gave you a freeway and open checkbook to solve Nicholas's problem and all I have seen are expenses without results."

Ronald opens his arms in bewilderment.

"Senator, you told me to wait for your orders. I put a plan to work. I just have to give the order and the Viking will be history."

Walter takes a deep breath and responds. "Then give the order right now, so I'll have to focus only on Charles. Another thing, make sure that there are no failures. I don't want to know anything about anything. "

Brandon tells Nick that being the first message to the nation after he officially entered the presidential campaign, it would be good if all the employees were behind him. Nick asks Roberto and Mark to take part, which they accept without a problem. Nick enters the office and asks Cristina to join the group, but she responds.

"Sorry, Nick, but I don't want to go out on social media. I left home to break ties with my family. I don't want anyone to see me and tell my mother. I don't want to end up with the peace of mind I have. I finally feel free and happy. You don't know what that means to me."

Nick replies. "I would like to have you in the group, but I respect your decision."

Cristina tells him. "Thank you for your understanding. I would like to talk to you about something today after the closing. It is something personal, so I prefer to do it when everyone is gone."

Nick worries, thinks that Mark has continued to harass Cristina and leaves the office totally tormented. Three hours later, Brandon, Namir, and Victor arrive to prepare Nick's message to the nation. Brandon tries to go over the message with Nick, but sees that Nick is totally unfocused.

"What's going on Nick? You made more mistakes than the words you said. Concentrate please, this is the most important message of all. Today you let the nation know that the moment of truth has come."

Namir interrupts. "Brandon, change of plans."

What's wrong? Brandon asks.

"Nick can't get on camera today. It would be a disaster. The public will think that when the moment of truth comes, Nick can't stand the pressure. No one will vote for a president who can't even withstand the pressure of a campaign."

Brandon asks. " What's going on Nick? Trust us; we are a team."

Nick could only think that if Mark had continued to harass Cristina, he would have to fire him. Mark had been working with Nick for twelve years and considered him family. It would be a very painful but totally necessary decision. Nick responds to the students.

"As you say, today is a very important day and I am not in a position to speak. There is a problem that has me completely unfocused. I can't help it. I will ask Cristina to record the message and so the three of you will be in the group."

Cristina cordially agrees to record the message. Brandon, standing in front of the group, heads to the nation.

"Citizens of this great nation. My name is Brandon, and I am the campaign manager of Nicholas Field, our Viking. We have once again shown that this is the country of freedom and opportunities. Where dreams become realities if there is a will and perseverance. What started as a spark turned into a flame, then they tried to put it out by blowing it, but they only gave it the oxygen to become an out-of-control fire. Now they can't put it out, it is too late because the fire is in the hearts of all the young people and citizens tired of the same thing. They never thought that a simple mechanic and a small group of students would put them against the ropes. But what they did not realize is that the simple mechanic represents the people of our country, and the small group of students represents youth and the future. Here we are, with you and for you. The future is yours and no one can take them away from you unless you allow them to take it away. Your vote counts and we count on your votes."

Cristina gave the phone to Namir, who uploaded it to social media. Brandon takes out a bottle to celebrate and when they raise the glasses, Cristina's phone rings. Cristina looks at her phone and excuses herself from the group.

"Sorry, it is the concierge of my building. I must answer."

Cristina separates and answers her call and then joins the group a little nervously. Mark looks at her mischievously. "What? Does the concierge make you nervous? How blissful that janitor is."

Mark's attitude confirmed Nick's suspicion, which disturbed him even more. After everyone left, Nick enters the office and sees that Cristina had changed her clothes. She is wearing a white blouse and a blue skirt.

"Are you partying?" Nick asks.

"It is my neighbor's birthday, and she invited me to her house. I tried to call her, but I locked my phone. Can you help me with that?" Cristina asks.

Nick picked up Cristina's phone, looked at it, touched a few keys, and said, "Your phone is not locked."

Cristina picks up the phone and says, "Then it's with me it doesn't want to work."

Cristina lowers the volume of the phone, dials three numbers and stares at the screen for about twenty seconds.

Nick bewildered looks at her and doesn't understand Cristina's attitude. Suddenly, Cristina throws the phone against the wall. Nick opens his eyes in surprise and before he can say or do anything, Cristina rushes towards him. Nick struggles to get Cristina off him. Help by advantage of the surprise factor, she hugs Nick. Nick pushes out Cristina, but Cristina scratches his face and arms. Cristina had kept screaming all along like a madwoman.

Nick had fallen into the trap. Cristina had dialed the emergency number 911 and when the operator answered, she started screaming and threw the phone against the wall. The operator, hearing the screams, sent immediately units to the address shown in the cell phone GPS. Three units arrived on the scene in less than a minute. The officers found Nick outside the office. Nick calmly tells them. "My employee has gone crazy; she is inside the office."

The officers enter the office and find Cristine crying with her blouse torn.

Cristina crying tells them. "He wanted to rape me, I had to defend myself, I tried to call you, but he took the phone away from me and threw it against the wall, when he heard the police siren he ran out, I don't know where he is."

Because Nick was a presidential candidate and such a controversial figure, the police took all the precautions and handled the case as required by protocol. Cristina's blouse and phone were seized as evidence. The police examined Cristina's nails to determine if they had Nick's DNA. Pictures were taken of the scene, Nick and Cristina by the ID technicians. The physical evidence was clear and supported Cristina's accusations. The police arrested Nick and took him to the county jail, where they put him in a solitary confinement for his safety.

Nick made national news again, but this time the media was relentless with him. The Miami Herald wrote, "THE VIKING ERA IS OVER." The New York Times wrote: "NICHOLAS FIELD ACCUSED OF ATTEMPTED RAPE." The Washington Post wrote, "THE SHAMEFULL END OF NICHOLAS FIELD."

Reporters besieged Brittany at her job to where the company forced Brittany to take paid leave to avoid the hassle caused by reporters at the supermarket. Brittany spoke to the cameras to ask for respect and privacy.

"In our country, the citizens are innocent until proven guilty, but you, with your comments, are giving a guilty verdict and are contaminating the opinion of any potential jury."

"Do you think your husband is innocent?"

"Yes, I know my husband and he would do nothing like that. I also know my husband's enemies, and I know what they are capable of."

"Will you divorce your husband if he is found guilty?"

"The case of him being found guilty does not mean that he is. Many people have been convicted while innocent. I will be by my husband's side, whatever the verdict turns out to be."

"There is a lot of evidence incriminating your husband. Does that evidence mean nothing to you?"

"I think I answered that question. I just want to ask you to respect our privacy and my children. I ask you to do your job responsibly and to take into consideration the harm you can do if you act irresponsibly."

Brandon calls an emergency meeting to prepare Nick's defense plan. An enraged Stanley says.

"I told him he should have told me before he hired that young woman. I would have investigated her and maybe we weren't in this situation."

At the end of the meeting, Stanley rushes out to Nick's shop. Upon arrival, he goes directly to Nick's office and takes fingerprints in the glass that covered Cristina's desk; then he leaves in a hurry.

Brando releases a statement asking his supporters not to lose faith and that they will prove in court that Nick is innocent. That Nick asks for a trial immediately in front of a judge without the need of a jury. Many people saw Brando's message, but few believed it. In the polls, Nick went from a virtual tie in first place to the last.

Both venues claimed victory. Governor Charles would give Peter a firm handshake and say.

"I knew you would not fail me. You are the best. Now the stupid idiot wants a speedy trial without a jury. We must help him with that, so a judge will convict him right there."

Senator Walter gave Ronald a big hug.

"Always trust you and your abilities. Your plan was fantastic. Even if he says that she was the one who tried to rape him, it will be his word against her. And if he gets acquitted, there will always be doubt as a shadow that will disable him forever."

Ronald responds, "I told you; I was going to get rid of him once and for all. I think it will be good if you use your influence to have Nicholas' request for a speedy, non-jury trial accepted. You could influence them to put in a well-known judge who hates sexual offenders."

Walter laughs and responds. "You have a good point in that, otherwise the press would focus on us and not on that idiot. I'll get to work on that this afternoon."

Unintentionally, Charles and Walter worked the same goal separately. There were several people who credited themselves with the plan for Nick's downfall, but they never found out who the actual author of the plan was. Nick lost popularity in the presidential race, but public interest increased as Walter and Charles' television comments in favor of a speedy trial under the pretext of clearing up Brando's rumors that Nick would represent himself and come out innocent.

Stanley goes to visit Nick at the county jail and tells him to represent himself and he will know what to do it on the day of the trial. Nick disagrees with him.

"I'm innocent. I didn't do it. I do not know how I'm going to prove my case if it's her word against mine and all the physical evidence is in her favor."

Stanley replies. "Just rest and do not think about anything. The less you know, the better. If I do not tell you anything, it is because we fear they will take what you know through a drug or hypnotism. Soon you will have the trail and you will come home stronger than ever."

A month after Nick's arrest, a lightning trial is underway. The nationwide press and foreign press were in the county court to cover the trial. The judge was very strict, especially on matters of sexual crimes. His own daughter had been the victim of rape. In any other circumstance, the judge would have been disqualify from handling the case, but Nick represented himself and did not object to the judge. Walter and Charles saw the judge's acceptance as inexperience on Nick's part and the final nail to seal Nick's political coffin. The judge enters the courtroom, and everyone stands up. After sitting down, the judge says.

"Case number 22-35467, the state of Florida representing victim Cristine Jordan and defendant Nicholas Field, who has exercised his right to seek a trial without a jury and to represent himself, are present in the courtroom and we will immediately begin the trial. Defendant Nicholas Field stand up."

Nick stands up and the room despite being full kept complete silence. The judge tells him.

"You are accused of attempted rape, events that occurred on the twenty-fifth of April of this year. How do you plead?"

Nick responds firmly. "Not guilty."

Murmurs were heard for the first time in the room. The judge immediately puts order and says. "Counselor your turn."

The lawyer was the brightest of all prosecutors with an undefeated record. The lawyer stands up and says.

"Anthony Caesar representing the victim Cristina Jordan who is present in the room."

The lawyer continues to address Cristina. "On the twenty-fifth day of April, you were the victim of an attempted rape in your workplace. Can you identify the perpetrator?"

"Yes, I can."

"Then point it out and say your relationship with the perpetrator."

Cristina, with tears in her eye's points at Nick and says. "It's him and he was my employer."

The lawyer responds. "Your Honor, let it become clear that the victim has identified the defendant as the perpetrator of the charges."

The judge responds. "Be noticed, continue."

On the twenty-fifth day of April, the defendant told the victim to stay after all the other employees were gone because he needed to talk to her. The victim changed her clothes because that night she was invited to a party at a neighbor's house. The victim had a hunch that something was not right, that was based on the morbid way that the accused looked at her. The victim took her cell phone in her hand, as the defendant did not stop talking and continued to look at her disrespectfully. The defendant began rubbing his private parts and told the victim, "I know you want it, too." The victim tried to call an emergency line that is, 911 and that was when the defendant threw himself on top of her, took her cell phone and threw it against the wall. The communications center of the Police Headquarters in the city of Miami received the call. The 911 operator is present as a witness and ready to testify. We have the recorded call where the victim's screams for help are clearly heard. The operator tracked the location of the cell phone from where the call came from and immediately sent the three units closest to the scene. After hearing patrol cars approaching, he left the office and tried to present himself as the victim to the authorities."

The lawyer takes an envelope with Cristina's blouse and says.

"No matter what the defendant said or what he says now in his defense, the evidence is here telling us what really happened that night."

The lawyer gives the court officer the envelope to show to the judge and says.

"That's the blouse the victim was wearing on the day in question. You can see that the blouse is torn, and the laboratory identified the defendant's DNA in the victim's blouse.

The lawyer takes another envelope with Cristina's cell phone and says.

"This is the other evidence where it shows that the defendant took the victim's phone and broke it to prevent her from calling the police. They also found the defendant's DNA on the victim's phone."

The court officer takes the phone and transfers it to the judge. The lawyer pulls out another envelope and says.

"Finally, here are results from the DNA test that was extracted from under the victim's fingernails. They all match the defendant's DNA by verifying the testimony of the victim who had to defend herself to avoid being raped. This is also consistent with the photos taken of the victim that same night. You can see the marks left by the victim's nails on the face and arms of the defendant."

"Your Honor, all this evidence presents a chain of facts that leave the defendant with no reasonable doubt as the perpetrator of the crime. Thank you very much, Your Honor."

All this time Nick had been looking at a folder that Stanley had given him. The folder only had a few notes at the beginning, a memory USB and at the end, another note with some papers and a name.

The judge tells Nick. "Mr. Field is your turn."

Nick stands up and says. "I want to bring my first and only witness."

The judge says. "Very well. Call your witness."

Nick says. "I call Miss Cristina Jordan testify."

The courtrooms erupt in murmurs, and the judge immediately asks for an order. Cristina, surprised, looks at her lawyer, who sees no danger and beckons her to stand up.

Nick says. "I want to ask the alleged victim to say her full name."

The lawyer opens his arms in disagreement and says. "Your Honor, that question is irrelevant."

Nick responds. "You see it as irrelevant, but I don't, plus I don't see any harm in your client saying her full name."

The judge responds. "I'm going to allow it, but focus on the case and nothing to go around it."

Cristina responds. "Cristina Jordan."

Nick instantly says. "Sorry, those people in the back did not hear you and you did not understand me. Please say your full name again."

Cristina turned pale and almost fainted. The lawyer, seeing Cristina's condition, quickly stops and grabs her arm. The judge also understood that something was happening.

"Are you Ok young lady? What happened to you?"

"I'm fine, your Honor. The mere fact of having to answer to this gentleman puts me in an uncontrollable state."

The lawyer intervenes. "Your Honor, it is common for victims to go into a state of shock when confronted with their perpetrators."

The Judge responds. "I understand. Please, Mr. Field, only ask the necessary questions."

Nick responds. "It's an extremely important question. Is she going to answer it or not?"

The enraged judge tells him. "She already answered. She doesn't have to repeat it."

Nick responds. "Very well, your Honor. That day we were celebrating, and the alleged victim received a phone call; she went to answer it at the office."

The lawyer stands up and visibly angry responds. "You Honor, the defendant is still going around in a circle with irrelevant statements."

The judge tells Nick. "I will not repeat that you must concentrate on the facts, that the young lady wants to answer a call in private. It is not a crime, nor is it relevant to the facts."

Nick introduces the USB and says. "Here, I present my evidence."

The confused judge asks. "What evidence is that?"

Nick responds. "Your Honor, a few months ago, the students who are managing my campaign gave me a clock."

The annoying lawyer stands up and says. "Are you going to allow the defendant to continue to say inconsistencies and irrelevances, disrespecting the court?"

Nick responds. "If you let me finish, then you will see the relationship to the case."

The angry judge responds. "Mr. Field, I am aware of the entanglements that you usually make in court, and I assure you that in my room, that will not happen."

Nick responds. "You are right, your Honor, but all those entanglements at the end I have untangled them, and the alleged victims have gone straight to jail."

The courtroom bursts into laughter and the enraged judge stands and says. "You are dead wrong with me. One more laugh and I will order to vacate the courtroom."

At that moment, everyone is silent, and the judge says. "Go on, but one more mistake and the trial ends here and I don't see it very much in your favor."

Nicks continues, "I had no knowledge that they had put a camera inside the clock. They never told me because they knew I would refuse it, but I must give them credit for seeing far beyond what I could see. Here you can see what actually happened that night."

Cristina faints, and the judge stops the trial for a moment. When Cristina comes back to herself, she says. "I'm sorry, but I can't relive what happened that night. I prefer to wait outside."

Nick instantly says. "I'm sorry, but if you leave this room and you're not accompanied by a court officer or a police officer, we'll never see you again."

The lawyer replies. "Isn't enough that the young woman was the victim of a rape attack, now we are going to victimize her again in court. I ask you to shield her from seeing that evidence if it is indeed evidence."

Nick responds. "Your Honor, the lawyer presented several pieces of evidence which were related to that night and did not have any effect on the alleged victim, but when I go to present mine, everything is different."

The judge worries. Could it be possible that will happen what he said that under no circumstances he would allow to happen? "I will allow and review the defendant's evidence."

Cristina hearing that he will allow the evidence whispers something to her lawyer. The lawyer stands up and says. "We can't accept that evidence. Revealing the contents of my client's phone call in the office violates her privacy as it was recorded without her consent."

Nick responds. "No problem. If she wants, we will take away the volume and no one will have to know that she received orders to accuse me of attempted rape."

When the judge heard what Nick said, his attitude totally changed, and he says. "Miss Cristina, if you don't want to see the evidence of the defendant, then you can wait in my chamber in the company of the court officer."

Cristina didn't respond, she just cried inconsolably. The judge placed Nick's USB on the TV monitor and horrified saw that Nick had again been the victim of unscrupulous enemies. When they finish watching the video, Cristina's lawyer says.

"Your Honor, I ask that all charges against the defendant be dismissed, and I ask that the alleged victim, Cristina Jordan, be taken immediately into custody."

Nick responds immediately. "That will not be possible."

The judge responds. "Why isn't it going to be possible? Are you going to defend her now?"

"No, Your Honor, because Cristina Jordan disappeared in Oklahoma nine years ago after reporting her stepfather for sexual abuse. The one you can take into custody is Sofia Bell, a theater student, a very good one by the way who lives in New York City. My security chief is a retired police captain." Nick points to Stanley, who stands up. "He took the fingerprints of the supposed Cristina and ran her in the national database. Here you can see the photo of the supposed Cristina. In reality, is Sofia Bell. That photo was taken the day she was arrested for driving under the influence of alcohol."

Nick gives the photo with the fingerprints to the lawyer, who looks at it and moves his head between amazement and embarrassment. The lawyer gives the documents to the officer, who passes them on to the judge. The judge examines the documents and puts both hands on his head and says. "My God, this is too much."

Nick responds. "Don't panic, your Honor, that there is still more come."

The room bursts into laughter and this time even the judge herself laughs. Nick pulls out some documents and says. "Miss Cristina, or rather Sofia, worked in my shop for eight dollars an hour, but she was receiving a deposit in her account for five thousand dollars a week, and the day after my arrest, she received a deposit of twenty thousand dollars. What a coincidence! Don't you agree, your Honor?"

Nick goes to give the documents to the lawyer, who immediately responds.

"No thanks, I have already seen enough, give it to the Judge."

The judge analyzes the documents and retorts. "Miss Cristina will remain in custody."

Nick smiles and says. "No, your Honor, it's Sofia. Cristina is missing."

The judge looks at the court officer and says. "Roy, do me the favor and get Mr. Field out of my room sign the papers, and let him go. What a man to make entanglements."

Nick opens his arms in amazement. "What I've done is untangle this and put things the way supposed to be. I'll tell you what it was like the day I met her."

The judge made a scream. "Shut up and leave my room immediately."

Outside the court it looked like a popular party, there was music, banners everywhere. Nick's wife is interviewed by CNN. "How do you feel about the verdict?"

Brittany replies. "You are wrong, it was not a verdict, there was no trial here. Here, a conspiracy against my husband was unmasked. I always said my husband was innocent. My husband and I were not affected by what happened because we knew we would show the opposite, but substantial damage was done to our children and that leaves a mark forever."

Half an hour later, images of Nick leaving the court carried on the student's shoulders traveled around the world. Even a Norwegian reporter was in Miami trying to interview Nick. The interviews were one after the other. The trial was a masterful propaganda move on Brandon's part.

Mami Herald wrote: "CAN ANYONE STOP THE VIKING?" The New York Times wrote: "CONSPIRACY AGINST NICHOLAS FIELD UNCOVERED DURING HIS TRAIL." The Washington Post wrote: NICHOLAS FIELD TEARS APART THE ALLEGED HERMETIC CASE AGAINST HIM, SENDS THE ALLEGED VICTIM TO JAIL AND TAKES AWAY THE LAWYER UNDEFITED TITLE."

CHAPTER EIGHT

The debate.

When the plot against Nick was uncovered during the trial and the masterful way he had defended himself, Nick's popularity doubled. The polls put Nick in the first place. This was more of a punishment to those who were playing dirty against Nick. At the headquarters of the Democratic Party, the leaders meet to analyze the situation. The leader of the Democratic Party tells Charles.

"I hope you had nothing to do with what happened in Miami, because the only thing they have achieved is to turn the voters against us and create distrust in the electoral process. The Green Party that never exceeded five percent is now at twelve percent. "

Charles responds offended. "Your comment is offensive and baseless. I don't care how much that jerk goes up in the polls, I tear him to pieces in the debate. He has reached that point because he has not had to answer questions where he has to show his knowledge of economics, international or domestic politics. In a debate in front of the cameras and without the support of his fanatical rabble, the Viking will go down in history."

The party leader responds. "I hope so, because if not, we are in deep problem."

Leaving the meeting with his party leader, Charles goes straight to his campaign headquarters where everyone was waiting for him. Charles angrily enters the headquarters and says.

"Peter, I want you in my office right now."

Everyone looks at Peter as the boy who is about to take a beating from his father. Peter takes a deep breath and responds. "Right away, sir."

Peter enters the office and Charles yells at him. "What the fuck did you do? Everything is under control, sir. From this one, he will not recover. My plan is perfect. That's not to mention the money you spent. If you had told me you were going to do that shit, I would never have allowed it."

Peter paled; his voice chokingly responds. "Governor, you told me you didn't want to know anything about anything."

An enraged Charles yells at him. "Pick up your things and disappear from here. I don't want to see you ever in my life. You're an idiot. Get out of here."

Since Nick had so many enemies at all levels of government, and at each of those levels, someone had taken the credit of imprisoning Nick to win points with the bosses. Everyone was to blame for the failure, but the person who did it was never identified.

In the Republican Party, Walter had moved to third place in the polls, with five points behind Gov. Charles. The leader of the Republican Party asks Walter.

"What plans do you have to regain lost ground?"

Walter responds by trying to downplay it but in reality, he was shaking inside. "There is no such lost ground. We are within the range of error and remember that the press pulls to the left, giving advantage to the Democrats."

The party leader asks him again. "So, you are not worried about this situation?"

Walter responds nervously. "No, I didn't mean that. I think the stupidity that the Democrats did trying to get rid of the Viking ended up hurting us all, but it's nothing we can't overcome."

"How do you know it was the Democrats who did that, if the same defendant says the person who paid her never identified himself and she has no way of identifying him?"

Walter even more nervously responds. "I deduce it, because I didn't and those behind us in the polls are too far away to spend such an amount of money to eliminate someone that they had no way to beat. Only Charles would have reason to do so. I don't have how to prove it, but it's very obvious."

"Yes, but that doesn't answer my question. What plans do you have?"

Walter responds. "It is very simple. We built a strong and experienced campaign. The current administration is a failure, and that is the end of Charles. No one wants the continuation of this failure. Regarding the Viking, he will fall because of his ignorance in the debate. As I understand, the furthest that poor man has ever left his house is to Disney Word four hours north of Miami. He has spent his whole life in his shop. He has a great merit for having come to where he is, but you have to be realistic he has no chance at all."

The party leader tells Walter. "You have a positive attitude and that's a double-edged sword, overconfidence is a dangerous thing. You can go now."

When Walter leaves, the party leader tells the others in the meeting room.

"If Walter fails us again, the only hope of taking the White House is by recruiting Nicholas Field into the ranks of our party. I want you to think about the best way to recruit him without making it obvious that Walter does not measure up to the task."

Walter knew he was in hot water and blamed Ronald for everything that had happened. Walter arrives at his headquarters and goes straight to see Ronald. Ronald sees Walter arrive and feels chills on his back. Ronald tries to get ahead and says.

"Senator, I need to talk to you."

An enraged Walter replies. "Are you going to present me another wonderful plan like the one that took the stupid to first place? The only thing you did right was that this young woman can't identify who recruited her and they can't involve us. No one has a sign on their forehead that says I'm stupid. That's why I made a deal with you, but if I make a deal with you again, it's because I deserve that sign on my forehead. I have nothing to talk to you about because you are no longer part of my team. If I see you at the headquarters, I will tell the authorities that I did an internal investigation and found out that you were behind the case. You will go to jail and maybe that will help me in the race. People will realize that I don't allow those things because I'm a man of principle. "

Nick's popularity grew so much that in every state in the country, you could see the vehicles with Viking's helmet. At universities, students wore T-shirts with Nick's photo with a Viking helmet. Nick came to merge in first place in the polls with five points ahead of Charles and seven points ahead of Walter. Both parties had hoped for the first television debate to be held in two months in Pennsylvania. The press besieged Nick and his family constantly, sometimes doing their job and sometimes with not very good intentions.

A reporter surprised Brittany with a cameraman broadcasting live for a national channel as she was leaving her job.

"Excuse me, Mrs. Field can I take two minutes of your time?"

Brittany knew that this moment would come eventually, so she faces the situation like a Viking.

"Yes, of course. What can I do for you?"

The reporter mockingly asks.

"Will you quit your job at Publix Supermarket if you become first lady?"

Brittany felt like sending him to hell, but she maintained a calm attitude and at the level of a true first lady who does not want to fall into provocations.

"No, when a person is used to working, to being productive, to contributing to his or her family and society, that person does not stop working for the simple fact of changing a social status. I will work on whatever I can to help those in need. I think it would be a great opportunity and a great honor for me to represent those mothers who like me work and are involved in the education of their children. I identify with all social classes because I come from the middle class and I do not hate the rich class. I am grateful and admire their entrepreneurial talent. I plan to ask for a leave of absence without pay for as long as I may be absent and then I will return to the life I have, the one I know and the one I am not ashamed of."

Brittany's response was so blunt that the reporter didn't know what to say. He had tried to ridicule Brittany, but he ridiculed himself in front of the nation. His face changed from defiant to ridiculed, and his cameraman couldn't stand the laughter at the sight of the reporter's face. Brittany, seeing that the reporter was mute, asks him. "Do you want to ask anything else?"

"No, thank you, that's all. "

Since the broadcast was live, and it was so clear that the reporter wanted to ridicule Brittany, this provoked the anger of women and feminists group attracting more supporters towards Nick's campaign putting him twelve points above Charles and thirteen points from Walter in the polls.

The long-awaited day of the debate arrived. It was the first time Nick had left Florida and boarded a plane. Brandon, Namir, Victor and Stanley accompanied him on the trip. The students had worked hard with Nick to prepare him for the debate, but they knew Nick was unpredictable and said things the way he sees it. They could get Nick into politics, but they couldn't make him a politician.

The experienced journalists, Jessica Johns, Barry Lee and Susan Black are moderating the debate in the auditorium of the Central University of Pennsylvania. Six candidates were attending the debate, but the focus was on Walter, Charles, and Nick. The audience practically ignored the answers of the other candidates and only paid attention to the answers given by Walter, Charles, and Nick. The debate remained cordial and half boring until Jessica Johns asked.

"Why you should be president?"

Charles responds. "The country knows my trajectory and experience. The state I rule has one of the largest economies in the world. I have been a support and advisor to the current administration. I know that many complain that the achievements of this administration may not have been as expected, but I must remind you that this is the product of what we inherited from the previous administration, where irresponsible spending and lack of planning for the future has forced us to take drastic measures. I promise that if I am declared president, we will see the fruits of our efforts, but if we deviate and forget all the sacrifices we have made so far, our children will pay the consequences of that mistake."

Walter simply turns to Charles and responds.

"Governor Charles believes voters are unaware of the disaster in this administration. Now he proposes the continuation of the disaster. The question is simple: are we better off than we were four years ago? If you are extremely rich, then you don't know or care. Excluding the extremely rich, we are all suffering. There is a wise proverb that says: IF IT IS NOT BROKEN DO NOT FIX IT. And that's what they did. If I am elected, I will return the country to the prosperity we enjoyed based on the basic principles of less government and more freedom."

Everyone was waiting for Nick's answer. It was the first question that tested Nick's potential. Nick calmly replies.

"If I am elected, I promise I will blame no one for the problems of my administration to conceal my mistakes. Obviously, none of you bring anything new to the table and only blame each other. That has been the constant in all the debates throughout the history of the politic in our country. No one admits their mistakes because they are the consequences of the previous administration. It seems that President Washington is to blame for everything."

The audience bursts into laughter and Charles interrupts and tries to ridicule Nick.

"You might believe that making the public laugh solves the nation's problems. That exposes the lack of seriousness you put into the debate and the future of the nation."

Charles' comments were like an order to shut up. Everyone was waiting for Nick's response.

"It's better to laugh with hopes of a better future than to cry with the threat of the disaster that you represent. How can you classify as an achievement to lead the country to an inflation not seen before? How can you describe it as an achievement to solve problems by printing money and causing the devaluation of the national currency? How can you speak of achievement when we were independent in energy and now, we are totally dependent? You have compromised the independence of our country; you cannot be independent if you are not self-sufficient."

The audience stands up, applauding Nick's response. Charles is speechless and doesn't know what to answer. Walter tries to capitalize by joining Nick and attacking Charles.

"I also applaud him; his response is in full accordance with our principles."

Nick looks at him and replies.

"I doubt it, Senator. You create the Chinese monster. You took the companies abroad to save money without caring that the working class suffered the consequences. With the money you have saved, China has bought half the world, including our country. If I am elected president, things will change. I will not sell the rope to the one who wants to hang me."

The audience again applauds Nick's response. Barry Lee asked the next explosive question.

Are you in favor of abortion?

Walter answers bluntly.

"Abortion is murder in any way you look at it. Many say that if a person was a victim of rape, they should have the right to choose an abortion That is punishing an innocent person for someone else's crime. We have institutions that can take care of those babies. There are laws in which a person can leave a newborn at a fire station without the fear of any charges. We adults must be responsible for our actions and not solve the problem by committing a murder."

Charles counterattacks Walter.

"I can see that you are not a woman. But tell me, can you look at that baby with the same mother's love when you know it was the product of rape? Do you think a woman deserves to live with that cross for the rest of her life? Do you think the answer is to give it to an institution and leave that woman with mixed feelings of guilt knowing that she gave her newborn to an institution and will never know about him or her again? I am a supporter of abortion and the women's freedom to decide about their own bodies."

Charles' response drew applause. Charles thought Nick would not answer such a controversial question.

"This is a very politicized question and a radical answer like the one from Senator Walter, or Governor Charles forget the rights and responsibilities of those involved in the case. It is totally inhumane and irresponsible to bring a child with physical disabilities into this world. If the parents want to have it, they are in their right and it is an admirable attitude, or perhaps selfish. What will become of that child when the parents are not there any longer? Denying abortion in that case can be a major crime, as we would force a person to live in a world that is by itself cruel. To live marginalized and in disadvantaged for a lifetime must be terrible. How great is the suffering of those parents who know that by the law of life, they will leave first and leave their child at the mercy of a stranger?

There is talk of a woman's right to have an abortion if she so wishes. Do men have no rights? If a woman fights with her partner and aborts, she is murdering the son of that man who must remain silent and see how she murder his son. Would you want to come into this world knowing that even your mother doesn't want you? I believe that instead of accusing each other, we should be more understanding and tolerant. I believe we must create the conditions to avoid these problems. We want young women not to have abortions, but we force them to go to a doctor to prescribe birth control pills instead of making them accessible in pharmacies. We want them not to have an abortion, but we bombard them with sex education at an early age and high sex content in the computer media. I believe that the pill that prevents pregnancy in twenty-four hours should be without prescriptions. I also believe that a person who, after knowing that she is pregnant, waits three months to decide to have an abortion is committing a murder. This is not black and white, this is living or dying. I will not give an answer like that to please a certain group."

No one applauded Nick's answer, but everyone knew it was the only sincere answer.

Susan Black asks the question that Walter and Charles were sure they would crush Nick.

What plans do you have to improve the economy?

Walter laughs and says. "Doing the opposite of what Charles proposes is enough. America became powerful by having freedom not only of speech and religion, but by letting the economy govern itself on the principle of supply and demand. The many regulations imposed by this administration slow down economic development and scare away investors. We have to reward companies by giving them concessions so that they can grow and, as a result, create jobs. Anyone thinks three times before starting a business because of government regulations. That fear will banish if we stop over regulation and grant government loans at low interest. The engine of the economy is in the medium-sized enterprise."

Charles takes off his glasses and cleans them, giving time to organize his ideas.

"Regulations are the result from the big companies abuses. When a worker feels protected, he is more productive, and more productivity equals a better economy. I don't understand how such a simple equation is so difficult for you to comprehend. In my state, we have created a just social system that allows workers to work worry-free and our state is one of the richest in the nation."

Charles' and Walter were short in their answers because they wanted to counterattack Nick base on his inexperienced. Nick looks directly at the cameras and responds.

"Economics is like the physical law of gravity. If you jump from a balcony, you will fall to the ground. I have a small mechanical shop..."

Walter interrupts. "I congratulate you, but you can't compare running a small mechanical shop to the largest economy in the world."

The audience laughs and reporter Susan Black says. "Senator, please don't interrupt. You already responded without interruption."

Nick responds. "No, it is the other way around. It's a good observation that shows how wrong Senator Walter is. It is the same to run a small shop or the largest economy in the world. If you mismanage it, you destroy it. You can't get more apples out of a barrel than the amount you put in. How can we improve the economy, if we're paying money to the people, not to work? I remember former President Obama saying it was Un-American and unpatriotic to put the country into debt the way former President Bush had done. At the end of the Obama era, the debt was even greater. Both Republicans and Democrats do the same and accuse each other. The current administration distributes and prints money as if that were the solution."

Charles tries to gain sympathy and ridicule Nick by saying.

"If I understand correctly, you believe that by eliminating social programs, we can improve the economy. Why don't you explain that to a father who lost his job and wouldn't get government aid to feed his family?"

Nick responds directly. "You take my words out of context and try to make believe that you are really interested in the people. I believe that anyone who has contributed and needs help should be helped, but that our country must import a workforce from abroad because its citizens do not want to work in the fields since they consider that work denigrating is unacceptable. We are paying for those who do not want to work and those who come to work send most of their salaries to their countries of origin. This process creates a society dependent on the government. You use these programs to intimidate those who receive it by telling them that if they don't vote for you, they won't get help. You create a dependent class which gets bigger and bigger in order to secure those votes. If we must import workers, you cannot say that we have unemployment."

Barry Lee interrupts and says. "We have to shorter our answers, time does not forgive. Many say our borders are insecure. What is your opinion and what do you propose?"

Walter did not waste a minute to criticize the current administration.

"The current administration has lost touch with reality; our country is being invaded. Such a violation of our country's sovereignty cannot be allowed. I propose to use the Army, if necessary, but we must restore order within our borders. I am not against legal immigration. We are a country of immigrants, but also a country of laws. "

Charles mockingly tells Walter. "Thank God that you at least say that you are not against legal immigration, otherwise North Korea would fall short of your measures. We are a country of immigrants, and we do everything possible so that those people who seek political asylum have their day in court, because as you said: WE ARE A COUNTRY OF LAWS. We do not have selective immigration as many would like, where skin color and language would be the dominant rule. I propose to strengthen the border and increase the immigration staff to speed up the process so that they do not separate these children from their parents. We still have children who, during the administration of former President Trump, were separated from their parents, and we could not reunify them yet. That is totally inhumane."

Nick looks at both candidates and shakes his head and says. "This is not a problem that started yesterday. The fault lies in both administrations. I remember that former President Ronald Reagan legalized ten million illegals and today we have twice as many again. Only during this administration, over five million has enter illegally. I believe that our country is being invaded by people who are being used by the enemies of our country. Twenty thousand people don't gather overnight to cross countries without having a leader, logistics and funding. Our country's enemies join human traffickers in creating chaos at our border. Who benefits from this? Well, believe it or not, not only the enemies who try to destabilize our country benefit, there are also people here who also benefit. Many make their money from the social plans provided to these refugees. When those who have nothing are told that if they arrive here, they will get everything; then it will be easy to concentrate thousands of people to go in search of the promised land. Those governments that do not care about their people feel great relief because it is less social service to provide to their citizens. They know they will receive a large amount of foreign currency when their citizens settle down and send money to their family. The Cuba communist government has organized a mass exodus every time it feels social pressure since the sixties of the last century. Only this year, after the protests that occurred on the island, more than one hundred and thirty thousand Cubans have entered through the Mexican border. It is a crime when children are left in the desert with only a phone number, knowing that they can die if border patrol does not find them in time. You take advantage of that to turn it into a political circus instead of investigating it and punishing parents for child neglect and abuse. They threw children as if they were packages from the top of the border wall without caring if you can suffer fractures that can leave them mutilated for the rest of their lives, but no one investigates. You say that there are children who have not been able to reunify them with their parents for years and I say that is a lie."

Governor Charles instantly sees the opportunity and interrupts. "How little you know about what you are talking, if you say that this is a lie! That's well documented. You should be a little more informed before you say something like that to the nation."

Nick responds to him on the spot. "No governor, it is you who must tell the nation the truth of what is happening and not deceive the people. What we have here are parents who don't want to hear from their children. A real father would be in front of the cameras claiming his children and not us looking for them to give them back. We also have people who buy or rent children to enter our country and then abandon them. There are the fingerprints of those people who entered with those children. I would look for them to bring him to justice. It is inconceivable how many

Haitians wait to cross the southern border on the Mexican side."

Charles saw an opportunity to attack Nick, but he remembered he had thought the same thing a few minutes ago and Nick practically mopped the floor with him, so he preferred to keep quiet. Walter, seeing that Charles had not intervened, thought it was a gift from heaven giving him the opportunity of a lifetime. Walter interrupts. "There are thousands and many nationalities south of the border, but Haitians are the ones who bother you the most. Justice cannot be just, if it is based on skin color."

Nick smiles, knows that Walter has swallowed the hook and will pay in the frying pan.

"Senator, I am totally with you. Haiti received an amount of money larger or equal to that used in the reconstruction of Europe after World War II. Where is the money? Are you going to tell me it wasn't stolen? Why isn't anyone from both parties accusing or investigating the case? The money that was supposedly used for the reconstruction of that small country was enough for its citizens to live in a super developed country. I am sure that the Haitian government is not the only corrupt one related to the disappearance of that money. Where is all the help the Latin America receives go? Their governments steal them and waste them, but that leaves a big question in the air: Why do you allow it? That puts you at least as accomplices.

If I am elected president, I will respect the laws of our nation and I will allow no one to enrich themselves with the pain of the poorest, and that includes those on our side. I will make sure that the aid to the people is for the people and no one else pockets it."

The audience stood up and applauded loudly. Charles felt great joy at seeing that Nick had destroyed Walter, that at least helped him. Walter cursed the moment he attacked Nick. The last question represented the last hope to Walter and Charles and even more luck because Nick had to answer before them. Barry Lee asks.

"Do you think America has lost ground in the international arena and what would your administration do to regain lost ground?"

Nick calmly replies. "My uncle retired from the US. ARMY after twenty-three years of active duty. I remember he could travel to any country only by presenting his military ID without having to use a passport. In those days, no one would dare to touch a citizen of the United States because they respected us as a nation. Today, that identification represents a danger to our security. Latin America has leaned to the left and is under Russian and Chinese influence. All this results from the weak politics of both parties and the support of corrupt governments. When the people suffer, it is very easy for the charlatans of the left to take a power base on false promises and then establish a dictatorship."

Senator Walter raises his hand and asks Nick. "Your intentions could be good, but your lack of knowledge is obvious and dangerous. Are you proposing that we intervene in foreign governments and install their presidents? In what century are you living in? To begin with, that is illegal and would be to serve our head on a silver platter to our enemies."

Charles smiles. He is sure that Walter has put Nick against the wall by calling him inexperienced and proving it by saying that what Nick proposed was illegal. Nick turns directly to Walter and replies. "Senator, you've been in politics for 30 years and apparently have a lot of experience."

Walter sarcastically responds. "Yes, I have enough experience not to say that we have the power to intervene in foreign countries as if we were the masters of the world."

Nick responds. "Let me remind you, Senator, that you were one of the most active in promoting the second war in Iraq, where the president of that country was taken out with cannon fire. You went on television saying that if you didn't act, Saddam Hussein would use weapons of mass destruction which were never found. I ask to give advice and help to opposition parties that have true democratic principles. To invest in a future of peace and prosperity. I propose that the countries receiving our aid should allow radio and television programs to inform the people about the progress made with this aid. That would prevent diversion of those funds and the peoples would see the benefits of those funds. No one leaves their place of origin if they are happy and safe where they were born. That would end the migration crisis and those peoples would have another opinion about us. No one would buy something of lower quality from China or Russia if they could buy it here. In transport along they would save at least twenty percent. We can regain the lost ground and expand our area of influence."

Walter, seeing that he fulfilled his goal, says. "If you believe in fairy tales, that's your problem, but here the reality is different."

Nick responds. "My theory is yet to be tested, but yours is the result of thirty-five years of failure, of which you are an active participant and directly responsible. The day I decide to be a failure, I will not hesitate to ask for advice."

The audience laughs and Charles can't help but laugh at the sight of Nick ridiculing Walter but decides not to say anything as a precaution. It's Walter's turn to respond, but after how badly Nick left him, he doesn't know how to start. Walter sweated and drank the glass of water with one shot without realizing that his body language and performance in front of the cameras portrayed him as a defeated man. Charles enjoys seeing a defeated Walter. He just had to shine in his turn and would claim a big victory.

Walter says pointing to Charles says. "The weak politics of the Democrats have led us to the current situation. Every time we make progress on something, and the Democrats take over the White House, they scuttle all the progress made. I will not go into detail about failures and just want to focus on the future. If elected president, I will put all my strength into regaining the prestige of our nation. I join former President Trump's motto: "MAKE AMERICA GREAT AGAIN." With a fair, strong, and firm policy, we will once again be the power we were. With your vote and your cooperation, this will be a problem of the past."

Walter's response was so short and without substance that they compared it to a boxer throwing in the towel. Charles felt a great relief. With Walter out of the scene, he just had to stay out of Nick's radar and not provoke him. Charles takes his time to organize his ideas without giving Nick or Walter a chance at a counterattack.

"We are certainly not the powerhouse we were a few years ago. I join my colleague Walter in not going into the search for a culprit and looking forward. If elected president, it will be a priority of my administration to strengthen relations with all countries. I will put all the experience gained throughout my thirty-three-year in politic into creating a team tasked to counter Russian and Chinese interference in Latin America. I will dictate the guidelines to follow. Throughout my career, I have taken part in many negotiations. Among all the candidates here, none can beat my record in representing our country in both trade and negotiations in conflicts of war. I don't want it to be misinterpreted that what I say this as an act of arrogance or down talking to lower the other candidates. They are all competent candidates, but my record speaks for itself."

Charles, emboldened to see that no one has attacked him and to prevent Nick from intervening, he tries to ingratiate himself with Nick saying.

"I want to express my admiration for Mr. Nicholas Field; he might not have a political career or experience in the international arena, but he has firm convictions. Nick, I need you in my cabinet. I'm sure the nation will thank and benefit from your energy."

With those words, Charles thought he had achieved his goal. He had said on camera that Nick was inexperienced and had praised him so that Nick would feel flattered and not attack him. Nick laughs and replies.

"Thank you very much, governor, but I don't want to belong to a team of losers. As you said, "RECORDS SPEAK FOR THEMSELVES." Like the disaster in Afghanistan, where the only thing that you accomplished was to arm the enemy to the teeth and abandoned Afghans that risk their lives working with us to their fate. Or perhaps when you attempted to send Iran, a terrorist country that has sworn to remove the state of Israel from the map, and clandestinely send a plane full of millions of untraceable dollars. You went with former President Obama to Cuba to establish relations with a country that has been oppressing the people for over sixty years, exporting revolutions and terrorism. Cuba paid for your gesture of good faith with a series of electronic frequencies attacks that damaged the health of our diplomats. Cuba's communist government said crickets produced those frequencies on the island. I did not know that in Cuba there was a brigade of anti-imperialist crickets that only attack American and Canadian diplomats. You have not done or said anything about it, and now the people took to the streets in Cuba for the first time in mass, the communist regime savagely repressed them, even imprisoning the children. After all this, you opened the American Embassy in Havana, increased the number of flights to the island and removed the limit of money that could be sent to the island. Your negotiation only gave oxygen to the dictatorship to stay in power, getting nothing in return. You are the perfect negotiator for the Castro's regime. As far as the domestic is concerned, during the presidency of former President Trump, we became energy independent, and you were the promoter of a policy that made us back energy dependent. Then went to negotiate with the cartel government of Venezuela to ask Maduro, who is not recognized as a legitimate president, knowing that there is an arrest warrant and a reward of five million for his capture, to sell you oil. Rightly so no one respects us."

The audience stood up and applauded for nearly five minutes. Charles was on the verge of fainting, cursing the moment he tried to ingratiate himself with Nick. Charles felt a lump in his throat choking him and swallowed the glass of water almost as Walter had done a few minutes before. Before the debate ends, they give members of the public the opportunity to ask the candidates questions. A young man tells Nick.

"My name is Joseph Clemente. New York City is where I live. I'm thirty - two years old. I have two children and I've been unemployed for the last three years. What can you do to help me?"

Nick exclaims. "Wao! That's a question that will take me time to answer. I prefer to pass the question on to my colleagues while I organize my answer. I need to know your full name and your date of birth."

Joseph bewildered asks. "Why do you want a date of birth?"

Nick responds. "Don't worry, it's to know your zodiac sign and give yourself an answer designed for you."

The audience laughs and Charles sees the last hope of regaining lost ground and ridiculing Nick.

"I didn't know you were a witch, and you need zodiac signs to give a simple answer."

Nick makes a signal with his arms like the one who reverently allows you to pass and responds.

"Go ahead, if you know how to help this young man, because I still don't know."

Charles responds. "I am going to implement the social programs that have given us so much success in California. Your children should not be collateral damage of the unpleasant situation you are going through. My programs provide training in many areas to prepare you and be competitive in the workplace. Our youth is the most valuable thing in our society, and we cannot look for the answer in zodiac signs. The answer does not come from heaven, the answer must come from us in whom they have put their vote and their trust."

Charles drew some applause from the audience and momentarily ridiculed Nick. Walter is sure that Nick is no match for this question. He should just humiliate Nick a little and give a better answer than Charles and will be back on track. Walter asks Nick.

"Are you ready to answer, or do you need more time to consult your zodiac?"

Nick responds. "No, neither the zodiac signs nor my decks of cards have been able to give me an answer, but maybe after you finish, some Viking sorcerer will enlighten my brain."

The audience laughs and Walter sees the green light for his rematch.

"I understand the situation is comical, but I assure you that this young man, like anyone who is in the same situation, does not find it that way. I assure you that under my government they cannot exist because I will legislate a law where, at the end of the last month of the unemployment payment, that information must be sent to the employment agencies. Employment agencies should give priority to these cases. I will give incentives to companies that employ these people. Governor Charles thinks that giving money solves problems, and it is quite the opposite. The young man has said it clearly. He needs a job now. While working, the person can learn and progress. The most important thing is that it is producing, and that raises his self-esteem. The answer is not to give money and create a dependence on the government. These expenses must be paid by the taxpayers and that creates another problem. I agree with Governor Charles. We also can't look for the answer in zodiac signs or black magic."

Although Walter's response was more logical than Charles's, he did not get any applause. It was as if he had something that did not fall into grace before the audience. Brandon and Stanley had prepared Nick for an answer like this. The trick was for Nick to get the full name with the date of birth, then he should buy time for them to research everything available in social media and public records. They would send all that information to Nick in a text message to answer the question.

Nick takes out his cell phone, puts it in the pulpit, raises his hand and says. "I have the answer."

The audience laughs and Charles, trying to prolong his streak of good luck, says.

"You live in Miami where Cubans and their Santeria religion abounds. Do you consult with the Babalao and Santero as well?"

The audience laughs, and Charles also laughs, enjoying his minute of glory.

"Yes governor, I consult the zodiac sign, the gypsy who reads the cards, the black magic sorcerer and the Babalao, Santero and they all told me the same thing, with which I agree: WE CAN NOT HELP YOU."

Walter, as a scolding and to get noticed, says. "Mr. Nicholas, this is a serious debate. If you are incapable of answering the question, then keep quiet and do not disrespect the nation."

Nick responds. "No senator, you are wrong. That is the correct answer and not the one you expose."

When Walter heard Nick's answer, he hit back in his tracks and said to himself, "SWALLOW ME EARTH." He knew that Nick somehow came out on top and make a fool of them. Walter understood that this was the end of his campaign and resigned himself to hearing the answer and waiting for a miracle. Charles was also speechless. Nick was like a magician who, in front of everyone, took a rabbit out of his hat and nobody understood how he did it. Charles wondered, "What the fuck happened here? What I said and what Walter said is correct. What am I not seeing?" Charles knew that if Nick beat them to this question, it would be a disaster for him.

Nick, addressing Charles and Walter, says. "You laugh at me because I supposedly consult with my advisors to answer a simple question, when in fact that is the right thing to do. A good president is not the one who does not listen to anyone because, in his arrogance, he believes he has all the answers. A good president is the one who surrounds himself with the best advisers who have no conflicts of interest to listen to them, ask them questions and then decide."

Charles desperately interrupts. " You're going around to not answer the question."

Nick doesn't answer him and, looking at his text on the phone, continues.

"Joseph Clemente, you dropped out of school; you had your first child at eighteen. You had your second child in your twenties; they are both from different mothers and you never marry them. Both women have sued you because you do not contribute to your child support. You have been arrested three times for possession of narcotics. The last time was in the city of Miami Beach during the Spring Break festival.

No matter how many programs Senator Walter and Governor Charles make available, you are the one who has to take the first step. As the saying goes: YOU CAN TAKE THE HORSE TO THE RIVER, BUT YOU CAN'T MAKE HIM DRINK WATER. If you are not willing to change your behavior and take responsibilities in life and mature, nothing and no one can help you.

You have found enough money to travel from New York to Miami and buy drugs, but you can't give your children something to cover their basic needs. While Jamaicans travel from Jamaica to Florida to work in the sugar industry because we don't have a workforce, you travel from New York to Miami to party and to buy narcotics. If you decide to change, I assure you that you are in the best country in the world to do so. I do not understand when this country has a labor shortages, a young and healthy person can say that he has been unemployed for three years. Both Charles and Walter immediately focused on the symptoms without analyzing the causes, perhaps because of their over experience."

The audience erupts in laughter and applauses. Walter and Charles only think about how they will face the leaders of their parties. They claimed the Viking ship would sink in the first debate and Nick had swept the floor again with the two of them." Nick comes back and says.

"Friend Joseph, if you decide to work, come to my small shop; I have an opening. The secretary who did my accounting got arrested for a false accusation, trying to remove me from the electoral contest. As you can see, my program is much more effective and faster than my opponents'."

The audience laughed and applauded, while Walter and Charles remained serious and did not dare to say a word. Nick continues.

"Every day when I was on my way to work, I would see an Anglo man of the few remaining in Miami standing on a corner with a sign in English and Spanish that said: HOMELESS, I NEED HELP." I several times gave him a dollar and I witness that the Latinos who passed by were very generous with him. One day, I thought about using him to paint my workshop. That day I rolled down the window and told him I had a job for him, and he said: LISTEN IDIOT, CAN'T YOU READ? THE SIGN SAYS I NEED HELP, NOT A JOB."

The audience laughed as if they were in a theater comedy. Nick continues.

"All the programs mentioned above have their merits. But the best program is the desire for improvement of the individual. In South Florida, we have two communities that are the perfect example of the above. The Cuban community is one of the richest communities and with the highest political representation in the nation. They came to our country without money and without the language; their achievement is the fruit of their hard work. The Haitian community puts an end to the myth of racism. The vast majority of them study and work hard. It is very common to see them in health care, earning a very good salary. Having a desire to progress and to contribute. Their concept of the family unity is an example to follow and the reason for their progress."

Joseph gets up and screams. "You have no right to violate my privacy and disclose my personal information in public."

Charles and Walter saw in Joseph the hope that someone could do something against Nick. Nick replies.

"You are wrong. I took everything I have said from the social media, which you yourself made public and government files, such as the criminal record that is also a public record. I have never divulged your medical record or your social security number. "

The election debate broke all previous records. Nick had given everyone a big surprise and on the streets of Miami, people went out in the street as they did the first time The Marlins won the baseball world series.

National television channels broadcast the celebration live on the streets of Miami and all the newspapers spread the news of the debate on the front page. The Miami Herald published photos of the celebration in the streets of Miami and wrote, "THE VIKING BOAT SINKS THE DEMOCRATIC BATTLESHIP AND THE REPUBLICAN BATTLESHIP ON THE NATIONAL DEBATE The Washington Post published the photos of Walter and Charles desperately drinking the glass of water and wrote, "THIS IS HOTTER THAN WE THOUGHT. " The New York Time published the photos of the bewildered faces of Walter and Charles and headed its editorial with the question, "WHAT HAPPENS NEXT?"

CHAPTER NINE

Meeting with Bill Ocano.

After the debate Nicholas did not return to the shop, because among the reporters and the curious, it was almost impossible to pass through the area. Reporters continuously besieged their home and his wife Brittany had to take time off from work. The school had to take special measures to protect Nick's children. Everyone's life had changed overnight. They had ceased to be an ordinary family and had become a celebrity, resulting in the loss of their privacy.

Nick meets with his team at his campaign headquarters to discuss the plan to follow. Brandon says. "I think you should go back to the shop, and we will continue as we have done so far. I don't see why change something that has worked so well. The image of a simple man in contact with the people has been what has put in the lead."

Stanley interrupts in disagreement. "I understand your concept, but you should understand that everything has changed. If before, when no one took us seriously, they attacked Nick in every way they could, now the road will be much more dangerous. We must increase the security; Nick can't keep walking around the city alone. I need three more people to reinforce security."

Nick, surprised, replies, "I think you exaggerate. Why do you want three more people?"

Stanley looks at him seriously and replies. "Nick, it's time for you to understand that these are the big leagues. We can't act like amateurs. I have two good friends in mind who retired from the police. One is Eric Wilson, a cybersecurity expert, and the other is Steve Donovan, an expert on terrorism and counterintelligence. The third would be to take care of the building at night."

The news of someone being hired to take over the networks did not please Namir, who felt pushed aside. Namir responds.

"I think then my services are no longer needed."

Stanley replies, "No Namir, quite the opposite. You are the leader of that department. He would take care of the security of our system to prevent cyber-attacks and to protect us from hackers."

Namir changed her expression, but she wasn't fully convinced. Nick steps in and asks Stanley. "Don't you think you are exaggerating? I don't think we need a specialist in counterterrorism and negotiations?"

Stanley replies seriously, "You have forgotten about history. Richard Nixon resigned for spying on the democrat headquarters. Someone assassinated John F. Kennedy. An assailant shot Ronald Reagan, and an assassin murdered Robert Kennedy during the presidential primary. These are the major leagues. If they tried to eliminate you without being a candidate, what makes you think things would be different now?"

No one could contradict Stanley; everyone knew things had changed. Nick asks, "Who would be the third to take care of the building?"

Stanley shrugs his shoulders and replies, "I don't have anyone in mind, but we need it."

Nick moves his head affirmatively and replies, "I want you to look for the security guard who was with you the night we met."

Stanley, surprised, replies, "Do you want the guard who wouldn't let you into the Democratic convention?"

"Yes, he was only doing his job. I have nothing against him; besides, he was the one who baptized me with the nickname of Viking." Nick replies.

Stanley addresses the group, "Please remember that this ceased to be a dream and has become a reality. This reality has its beauty and its danger. Let's enjoy the beauty without forgetting the danger. From today on, I will be Nick's driver and take him everywhere. I will tell Eric Wilson to start by putting a security system in Nick's house and when he is done, he will meet with Namir for her to show him our computer system."

Stanley addresses Brandon, "Brandon, you are to keep Nick's agenda?"

"Yes, I'm going to take care of keeping the agenda." Brandon replies.

"In that case, I need you to inform me in advance so that Steve Donovan will check the place and approve it if it is a safe place." Stanley replies.

Stanley's attitude was not well received by the students and Nick's himself. Stanley sees in everyone's faces that although no one contradicts him, they did not like it either. Stanley stares at them and says.

"I understand you see me as a stranger who arrives at the last minute and has given orders. Maybe if I was one of you, I would feel the same, but I don't try to tell you how to do your work. You have built this, and no one can deny it. The only thing I intend is to take care of your work so that no one can harm it. I also want to remind you that starting today, you are the targets of the enemies, and you must take great care of yourself. But if you think I'm overdoing in what I'm asking, I just leave and wishing you good luck. I can't do a half-way job; I will feel responsible if something goes wrong."

Stanley's words were clear and direct. The students and Nick understood Stanley was right, and that he was not trying to interfere, but to protect their work. Nick replies, "You're right and excuse us. This has been quick, so it's hard to assimilate."

The phone rings and Namir answers it.

"Headquarters of presidential candidate Nicholas Field. How can I help you?"

"Hi, I'm Bill Ocano, vice president of the Republican Party. Can I talk to Mr. Nicholas, please?"

Namir covers the headset with her hand and addresses the group. "I have Bill Ocano on the line. He wants to talk to Nick."

Nick replies, "Who the hell is Bill Ocano? Tell him we had the posters done with another company."

Namir answers the phone. "Mr. Ocano, Nick is not here just now; I don't know if he left. Can you wait on the line while I check if he is still at the headquarters?"

"Thank you very much, young lady."

Namir presses the mute button and addresses the group. "It's the vice president of the Republican party who wants to talk to Nick. What do I tell him?"

Everyone looks at each other waiting for someone to say something and when no one answers Nick asks Stanley. "What do we do?"

When Stanley heard Nick's question, he flushed, returning to his time as a in police sergeant, when he would scolds his officers. Stanley responds as a scolding.

"Brandon is the campaign manager. He must take that call. Nick, you oversee the approval of Brandon's decision and get ready that this is just the beginning. Hell! You have come this far without me; you don't need my advice. I'm just security."

Stanley's scolding put everyone back in their place and made them react. Brandon picks up the phone and answers.

"Good afternoon, Mr. Bill. Nick has just left. I am Brandon, the campaign manager. If you want to leave a message, I will gladly convey it to him."

Bill hears the young man's voice and tries to take advantage of him, knowing that the young man has no experience in politics. "Thank you, Brandon. I will give you my number for him to call me when he can."

Brandon responds bluntly. "I'm sorry, but he won't answer anyone's call if he doesn't know from whom and for what."

Brandon's response was so dry that it put Bill on the defensive. Bill knew that if he didn't get ahead of everyone, the Democrats could recruit Nick.

"Yes, of course. Tell him that Bill Ocano wants to meet him at the Hilton hotel in Miami."

Brandon thinks for a while. Everyone is paying attention to the conversation.

"If you wish, you can come to our headquarters and meet him tomorrow at two o'clock in the afternoon. That's the only space open for a long time."

Bill tries once again, "Perfect, then tell him we'll meet at the Hilton tomorrow at two."

"Mr. Bill, I think you didn't understand me. You can come to the headquarters tomorrow at two. Here is the place of your meeting."

Bill bit his tongue to restrain himself. A daring young man had treated him as if he were one of the bunch, but he had no choice.

"If I understand, I wanted to invite him to lunch while we were talking, but lunch will be another time. Tell him that tomorrow I will be at two o'clock at your headquarters. Thank you, very much young man. Have a good day."

Bill hangs up the phone and says, "Stupid brat. Who the fuck do you think you are?"

Stanley pats Brandon twice on the shoulder and says.

"That's how it's done, boy. They are the ones who must come to you. You don't know how proud I am of each one of you."

Everyone applauds Brandon, who still didn't come out of his amazement. He had put the head of the Republican Party in his place. It was obvious that the students were not prepared for such a task, but they had the talent and the will to move forward. Only Stanley saw the talent in them and was sure that Nick could be the future president, so he encourages him and raise his self-esteem.

"I know that for all of you, this new situation may create doubts about your ability to operate. When you started, it was easy and fun. There was nothing to lose. You enjoyed the triumphs without caring about a setback. Now that you are in the first place, the scenario has changed. Now, instead of attacking, you must defend yourself. Nick and you will receive attacks of all kinds, but I trusted that you have the talent and integrity to emerge victorious. We are a team and each of us is the best, that's why we are in first place. I only ask you to follow your instincts as you have done so far. It's better to make a mistake by doing something than to make the mistake of doing nothing."

Stanley's words had a great impact on Nick and the students who applauded and saw in Stanley the motivator they needed to move forward. Namir, who only a few minutes before had felt jealous and, to some extent, distrust

Stanley, hugged him and, with the tears of emotion, gave him a kiss on the cheek.

"Thank you for your words. That was the push we needed to not get stuck. We will move forward and be prepared for an impenetrable defense."

Victor says, "I'm sure Bill wants to get together to buy Nick."

"Very well thought out." Stanley replies.

The next day Nick was in his office at his headquarters waiting for Bill since one o'clock in the afternoon. He could not hide his nervousness and curiosity about the meeting. Bill arrived on time for the appointment and arrived in a relatively old and dirty car. Bill was wearing jeans, shirt and dark glasses. He didn't want to be recognized by anyone, especially the press. Victor greeted Bill, who did not know who he was.

"Good afternoon, gentleman. Who are you looking for?"

"My name is Bill and I have an appointment with Mr. Field."

Victor realized Bill didn't want to be recognized and replies.

"You can take off your glasses. Here, nobody is going to use your presence to blackmail you, or we are going to tell the press. We have principles and values; you can relax."

Bill would have preferred a slap; he took a deep breath, trying to control himself. He was not used to lowering himself, much less that a young man treated him that way.

"Oh no! It's that the Miami sun is unbearable. That's why I prefer to dress this way and wear glasses to avoid ultraviolet rays."

Brandon had listened to the entire conversation and introduced himself and also kick Bill in the stomach.

"Hi Mr. Bill, my name is Brandon. I'm Nick's campaign director. Welcome to our place. Don't worry about our weather; if you live in Miami, you will get used to it and enjoy it. They say that the sun punishes more the white-skinned people, so you have an advantage over us. None of us wear glasses unless we go to the beach, but of course, we are acclimatized."

Bill felt he had started with his left foot, because when he looked around, he was the darkest of all. Bill was about sixty-six years old, tall and mulatto; he didn't have a good sense of humor, so he was about to explode. Bill takes a deep breath again, counts to three and responds.

"You're absolutely right's all about acclimatizing."

Brandon accompanies Bill to Nick's office, opens the door without touching, and tells Nick. "Nick, here is your appointment for two o'clock in the afternoon."

Bill could not hide his amazement. The presidential candidate's headquarters was a warehouse run by inexperienced students, and Nick's office was so small that there was only room for a desk, two chairs, and a TV.

Nick gets up from his desk and shakes Bill's hand.

"Good afternoon, Mr. Bill, a pleasure to meet you. Please sit down."

Bill takes one of the two chairs in front of the desk and sits down. There was a hidden camera and microphone detector in Bill's portfolio. Bill puts the portfolio on his legs, waiting for the right moment to open it.

"I'm sorry you were so busy. I wanted to invite you to lunch at the Hilton Hotel. Your headquarters is small, but cozy. I brought you a letter from the president of our party. "

Bill opens his portfolio to see if his device had detected hidden cameras and microphones.

Nick notices Bill has not looked at him in the face as he spoke and had been sneakily looking for cameras and microphones hidden in the office.

"Mr. Bill, if your concern is that, if I have cameras and microphones in my office, the answer is yes. But you don't have to worry, they are just for security, not to blackmail anyone. I'm sure you know that a hidden camera saved me from going to jail for several years."

Bill felt a chill on his back. He hadn't won a single one since entering the headquarters. It was as if they could read his mind. Bill looks at his device and sees that it has all the red lights on. Bill closes the portfolio; he knows he must be careful with what he says and he cannot leave without saying what he came to say.

"What a memory I have! I brought a letter and left it at the hotel. Actually, it does not matter so much, because I can transmit the message to you myself. We are impressed with your work. You have proven to have the values and principles that identify with our party. Unfortunately, in our ranks, there is no one who can get even close to you. We want to extend you an invitation to be part of our party and in that way be able to give you the logistic and economic support you deserve. If you and I agree on one thing, it is that the current administration is a disaster, and we must come together to save the country. You would be the official candidate for our party. You remind us of Donald Trump. Like him, you are a political phenomenon. You also sound like him; that's why I am your number one fan."

Nick raises both hands, signaling Bill to stop. Bill stops abruptly.

"Sorry Mr. Bill, but don't compare me with Mr. Trump; I am not a fan of Mr. Trump, I am not like Mr. Trump, and I don't want to be like to Mr. Trump. Mr. Trump is a narcissistic, egocentric, arrogant, disrespectful, and conceited. He once said that he could shoot somebody on the street, and they still will vote for him. That is the same as calling the people stupid. He said that he could run against George Washington and Abraham Lincoln and beat them. That is such a disrespect that makes me sick. I must admit, he is an excellent administrator, but nothing else. Now, putting Mr. Trump aside, can you tell me what does Senator Walter say about this? Does he know you are betraying him?"

Bill worries, if this video comes out, it would be an enormous scandal, but there is no going back.

"Unfortunately, Senator Walter has not lived up to our expectations, and you are wrong. It is not betraying

Senator Walter; this is putting the well-being of our nation above anything."

Bill handpicked his words so he could defend himself in case Nick would leak the recording of the meeting to the press.

Nick asks, "What is this the purpose of our meeting? Do you want me to abandon those young kids and go with you? That I betray all those who have supported me unconditionally."

Bill moves his hands to a stop, as if trying to deny what Nick said.

"No, no, no way, you have misinterpreted me. Those young kids will come with you. They will replace Walter's team. Breaking up your team would be a serious mistake. These young kids have a bright future at our party."

Nick shakes his head in bewilderment and responds.

"I'm sorry, Mr. Bill, but I can't accept your offer. I owe it to those who supported me because they saw in me a hope, not a party. Do you truly believe that I am qualified to take the reins of our country and ensure a better future than Senator Walter or Governor Charles can offer?"

Bill responds immediately. "I'm convinced of that. That's why I'm here. The future of our nation is at stake."

"Are you putting the interests of the nation above those of your party? And you don't regret it?" Nick asks.

"I do not regret it; it is the duty of every worthy citizen to put the interests of his country above his own interests."

Nick gets up from the chair and shakes Bill's hand. "You don't know the pleasure it gives me to hear something like that from you."

Bill feels great relief. He thinks he has convinced Nick. "The pleasure is mine to know that we are both on the same side."

Nick adds his left hand and shakes Bill's hand with his two hands, "If your main interest is the future of the nation, it will be a great honor and it will help us a lot to have you among our ranks, welcome to our group."

Bill felt as if someone had thrown a bucket of cold water on his back and stutteringly responds. "No, don't misinterpret me, please. I haven't said I want to leave my party. My intention is for you to join ours."

Nick withdraws his hands and sits down. "In this case, we should end this meeting. It has been a pleasure to meet you."

Bill understands he must use other methods to achieve his goal.

"Mr. Field, I can give you ten million reasons. It would be beneficial for you to join our ranks."

Nick throws his head back and raises his eyebrows in amazement. "Just give me only one reason that convinces me, and that will be enough."

Bill stares into his eyes and slowly replies, "A wise man can read between the lines."

Nick responds bluntly, "I'm not interested in your reasons. You have spent over a hundred million reasons on your campaign and are lagging in third place. As you can see, your reasons don't convince voters."

Bill tries once again. "Mr. Field, it is possible that you will win the presidency, but you could not govern, you would have Republicans and Democrats against you, the country would stagnate and bring chaos of incalculable consequences. Everything I do is for the good of the nation. If you do not want to join our party, I can give you many more reasons to give up the race, in this case twenty million reasons to save the country."

Nick stands up, walks to the door, and opens it and says, "Good luck to you, Mr. Bill, and I'm not interested in one, or twenty millions of your reasons. You know where the exit is. The place is not that big and you can sleep peacefully. Our meeting is confidential."

Bill leaves in a hurry without saying a word. Brandon asks.

"What does he want?"

Nick, as if nothing had happened, responds. "Offer me five million dollars to move to his party, but I refused; then he offered twenty million to leave the campaign."

"Mamma Mia!" Namir exclaims.

Nick laughs and replies, "I'm sorry, but you're going to have to stick with your old Toyota."

Two days later, Bill meets at the Republican Party office. Everyone was eager to know the outcome of their encounter with Nick. Bill had come out of the meeting with Nick so demoralized that he hadn't communicated with anyone in the office. Bill walks in and looks around and sees his office on the top floor of an upscale building with a panoramic view of the city. They all are wearing expensive dresses in the latest fashion. Bill wonders how it is possible that students and a stranger have been able to push him to third place with virtually no chance of winning the presidency. Maira, the finance secretary, tells him, "We thought you had stayed on vacation in Miami. You didn't even answer the phone. What good news do you bring us?"

Bill responds. "I have good news and bad news. Which one do you want first?"

Maira responds with a smile, "I prefer the bad first, so the good one eliminates the taste of the bad."

Bill responds reluctantly and slaps the table.

"The bad one is that we're screwed, and the good thing is that they will not accuse us of bribery."

Everyone looks at each other. Bill was a formidable negotiator, capable of convincing anybody.

"Since I entered their headquarters, they shit on me, ridiculed me, and practically kicked me out. Then I was waiting for the scandal in the press, but at least he kept his word not to leak our interview."

Bill looks around and sees that everyone is quiet and surprised. "There is no diplomatic arrangement here with that Viking and his crew of brats. We have to solve it in another way. We have no choice but to continue with the stupid Walter and hope for a miracle. "

Governor Charles, seeing that the polls kept him in second place, but without advance and far behind from

Nick, contacts his friend Cristian Berry, a journalist who works for a national network. Charles meets with Berry at a Los Angeles restaurant to ask for a favor.

"Cristian, I need a big favor from you. Nick has turned out to be very good at debate, but I don't think he has the intelligence to answer questions if he's surprised, let alone live on the national network. Florida is very important, and the Cuban/Venezuelan vote is almost decisive. If you put that vote against Nick, I can secure Florida because Broward County and Palm Beach are Democratic. I assure you that this favor will not be forgotten. I will be indebted to you. Just look for two questions that put him against the wall. Hunt him down when he leaves his headquarters so he will not have time to think or have anyone advise him. If he decides not to answer, then he will show that he is not prepare, and that he is betraying the Latinos. I'll take care of the rest."

Cristian remains thoughtful. He knows that if Charles becomes president, he could collect the favor as a White House correspondent. "I think I can help you. I will tell my boss that I have got an interview with Nicholas Field. I'm sure he will accept because he knows it will bring a large audience to the channel, but I need you to spy on the headquarters and have the time when he leaves the headquarters. Only in that way I can tell my boss that I will do a live interview at a certain time."

Charles feels a great relief and replies, "When I have that information, I will communicate it to you immediately."

Charles hires a private investigator and sends him to Miami with the task of spying on Nick's itinerary. After a week, Charles contacts Cristian and gives him the information that Nick arrives at the headquarters every day at 8:30 AM and leaves at 7:30 PM. Cristian leaves immediately for Miami and takes Nick by surprise on a Friday when he exits the headquarters because that way, he would have a greater audience and Nick would be tired after a week of work.

Cristian besieged the headquarters like a tiger to his prey. Since it was Friday, the students had left early and there was only one car left in the parking lot. Cristian knows Nick had not left yet, so he parks his van at the headquarters' parking, pulls out the antennas are ready to transmit live as soon as Nick gets out of the building. Cristian's plan had gone perfectly, at least as far as the time coordination was concerned.

Nick and Stanley leave the headquarters and are surprised by the lights of the camera. Before they have time to react, they hear to the words of Cristian Berry.

"This is NNC broadcasting nationwide live from Nicholas Field's headquarters. I am Cristian Berry, and I have the honor of interviewing Nicholas Field for you."

Nick understands that since it is a live transmission, refusing to be interviewed will be a big mistake and a show of weakness. Nick also concluded that Charles could only orchestrate this, as he was the only one who had a chance, even though remote, to compete in the campaign. Stanley looks at Nick, waiting for Nick's order, but Nick steps forward and responds with a question.

"Is this a live transmission?"

"Yes, it is Mr. Field. The people listen to you."

Nick moves his head affirmatively and smiles, "Thank you so much for the opportunity to reach out to the people. This is not only a live interview but also an interview where I have been caught by surprise leaving my headquarters. I don't want to waste the opportunity to reach so many homes and is free. I don't have the money to make such a campaign ad, but I see my opponents collaborate with me in this, so I want to thank them for such a gift."

Cristian closes his eyes and swallows. Nick had exposed Cristian to his boss, but it was too late; he had to continue with the plan.

"Mr. Field, voters are concerned that you are committed to the Cuban and Venezuelan vote. They think you're going to send the Marines to free them from those dictatorships. What's true about that?"

"I don't know where you get that information from. First, that's false. Second, the life of one of our Marines is as important as that of any Cuban or Venezuelan citizen. I know that generalizing is not fair, because you will always offend or be unfair to someone. I would never turn my back on people who rise and fight for their freedom, but neither would I send our young people to die for the freedom of those who do not free themselves. The Cuban dictators remain in power mostly because of the billions of dollars sent by the same ones who ask for political asylum in our country, they take advantage of all the government aid, but a year and one day after their arrival to this country, they return to Cuba loaded with suitcases. I never heard that a Jew fled Nazi Germany and came back to Germany after a year and one day. There are members of that community of impeccable conduct, and I apologize to them. My comments may be offensive to some, but they are true for all.

Regarding Venezuela, I believe that the so-called opposition is as fraudulent as the Maduro dictatorship. How can an assembly of an absolute majority never remove a fraudulent president who is proven not to be born in Venezuela? They never even mentioned the case. They deceived the people with the recall referendum which never put it in place. Finally, when the entire world gave full support to Juan Guaido as president and ignored Maduro, he negotiated with the dictator. Enrique Caprioles betrayed his people when he won the elections and the people wanted to take to the streets to defend the vote; Capriles told them to go home, that the dictator will recount the votes. The wolf would take care of the sheep. Do you think our soldiers should die defending something like that?

What I can tell you is that I would never betray young people like those of the Arab Spring who were savagely repressed by Iranian tyranny and President Obama left them to their fate and then rewarded the tyranny by trying to send a plane loaded with our taxpayer's cash. I should ask Governor Charles, who was active during that administration, why he did not speak out on the matter."

Cristian asks his second question by trying to present Nick as a controversial candidate who would bring only trouble should he take power.

"Many believe that by running as an independent, you will not have the help of both parties. History has shown that both the Senate and Congress punish the opposing party with their votes. You have caused several headaches at both parties. If you take power and both Republicans and Democrats decide to take revenge on you, your government will stagnate and would practically be a misrule for four years."

"Are you saying that members of Congress and the Senate put their ego above their duties to the nation? Because I don't think so; I believe that both the Senate and the Congress are composed of people elected by the people to represent them and will not disappoint them by obstructing the progress of the country. I am sure that we have people who dedicate to serve the people and are loyal to their president whatever their party affiliation. Every senator or congressional representative takes an oath to serve their constituents, not the party. And finally, you are wrong, I am not an independent candidate, because independent means I do not answer to anyone. I depend on and belong to the people." Nick pauses and says out loud. I AM THE PEOPLE'S CANDIDE. Thank you very much and God bless you all.

Nick's interview took everyone by surprise and once again Nick came out on top. For Governor Charles, things went the other way, as the owner of the NNC channel realized that the host of his channel, Cristian Berry, had deceived him by telling him he had a scheduled interview with Nick. The owner of the NNC channel, Mr. Dan Suao, was very strict and the policy of his channel was to remain objective and impartial. This policy had given him excellent results, because most of the national channels were inclined to the left, favoring the Democrats and Fox

Channel leaned to the right, trying to counter the other channels and favoring the conservative Republicans.

Dan Suao walks into his office, picks up the phone and calls his secretary, "Good morning, Martha, I need you to contact Cristian and the cameraman who accompanied him to Miami; tell him I want them as soon as possible in my office."

Martha replies, "The cameraman is Juan Yera. He is in the studios right now. I saw him about twenty minutes ago. Cristian comes in two hours; he's going to edit some recordings for the 7:00 PM newscast."

Suao responds softly, but firmly. "I want Juan Yera in my office now and give Cristian a call to come immediately. Please also call the reporter covering Cristian's vacation and tell him he will have to cover Cristian's space until further notice."

Martha says goodbye to Suao, hangs up the phone and grimaces in terror and moves her hands like if she has touched a hot iron. Martha's companion, seeing Martha's gestures when she hung up the phone, asks her. "What happened with the boss? Don't tell me he will get on Cristian's case because of the interview."

Matilda, Martha's partner, was a Democratic activist, but she was wise and respected the rules of the channel. She only made small comments to Martha because of the trust they had with each other.

Martha replies, "Ha, ha, ha. The old man is blown up like a coffee maker. As always, he remained calm, but I assure you he's blowing smoke through his nose and ears."

Matilda says reluctantly. "Actually, Cristian raised the audience for the channel a lot with that interview and as always, everyone who relates to that son of a bitch Viking is burned. If that man wins, he will start the third world war."

Martha communicates with Juan Yera. "Juan, the boss wants you in the office; leave everything you're doing now and go to his office."

Juan exclaims. "I knew this was going to explode. It was a matter of time. How is the boss?"

Martha, despite being an older person, had a great sense of humor and was known for her sayings and occurrences. "He's very calm, but if I were you, I would put a pillow in my ass before I go to see him."

Juan was one of the oldest cameramen in the station; he and Suao had a friendship that went beyond work. Juan enters the office and sees Suao sitting at his desk with an unfriendly face. "Good morning. Martha told me you wanted to see me urgently."

Suao stares at him without saying a word and with his right hand tells him to sit down. Juan sits down and knows that the situation is hotter than he imagined.

"How many years have we known each other?"

"Over twenty-five years. I was your second cameraman. The channel was only one year old. I had come from Puerto Rico; I was desperately looking for a job and you gave me the opportunity." Juan answers.

"I'm glad you have an excellent memory. Now, what has been the motto of our channel from the beginning?" Asks Suao.

"Objectivity, Integrity and Impartiality above any interest." Juan responds by trying to guess where Suao's scolding would come from.

Suao points his finger at him and says, "You were here in my office with Cristian when he asked me for permission to take you to Miami with him because Nicholas Field had granted him an interview. You lied to me, and I want to know your participation in this."

Juan embarrassed, lowers his head and replies, "I didn't lie to you. I believed Cristian when he told me that Field had granted him an interview. I saw this as a big stroke of luck for the channel, and it was. When we arrived and went to the headquarters, it surprised me to be in a parking lot near to the headquarters. I thought we were early for the appointment, so I didn't pay attention to it. Then, seeing that an hour had passed, I asked Cristian at what time was the interview and he evaded the answer. Cristian's cell phone was on top of the van console when he got a call; I saw that the call came from Charles. Cristian quickly picked up the phone and got out of the van to answer. That's when I realized we were on the lookout for Field and we didn't have any appointments."

"Why did you film the interview if you knew it wasn't approved by me, nor was it right what you were doing?"

Juan moves his head, squeezes his lips, and takes a deep breath. "I didn't dare to say anything, because Cristian is superior to me, and I also thought it would be an outstanding achievement for the channel. In fact, the numbers showed it was."

Suao stares at him and replies, "I don't blame you for going to Miami. You also believed the story that Field had granted the interview, but two days have passed since the interview, and you never told me what happened. That makes you complicit and goes against the integrity, loyalty, and honesty that I expect from each of you. If you had informed me of this when you arrived, I would not have you here in front of me today. Believe me, I don't like this at all, because you are a little more than an employee to me. I think there is enough confidence between us."

Juan reddens and replies, "You're right. I should have informed you, but I've been working with Cristian for twelve years and it was very uncomfortable for me to give him away."

Suao moves his head up and down as if he agrees with Juan, "All right, then you owe more loyalty to Cristian than to me. You have known him for twelve years and have known me for twenty-five years, plus I am your and Cristian's boss. You are an accomplice by not informing me, so you are suspended from employment and salary for a month. If it seems unfair to you, tell me and expose your defense."

Juan knew Suao separated friendship from work, especially to discipline someone, so he wasn't entirely surprised. "No, I know. I committed a fault and I accept the consequences; I want you to know that it doesn't change at all on my side the friendship and gratitude I feel for you."

Suao smiles and replies, "You better, old fox, and I warn you I would never forgive you if you do it again. You can leave and lie to your wife, tell her I forced you to take a vacation."

Juan answers. "And the check? How do I save myself from that one? You know she's the one who makes all the payments."

"That's your problem. Go see what you can come out with, but don't count on me to lend you a penny." Suao replies.

One hour later, Cristian bumps into Juan in the channel corridor; they just say good morning, but Cristian understood everything that's going on just by seeing Juan's face. Before entering Suao's office, Martha asks Cristian.

"Did you use the channel's cell phone in Miami or before in something related to Field's interview?"

Cristian shakes his head in desperation. "Shit! Don't tell me he asked for the phone records."

Martha moves her head affirmatively, "Yep! Same day, he asked them for the last two months. That is why it has taken him two days to call you to his office. That old man doesn't miss one, so don't try to be a smart ass or you're going to make it even worse."

Cristian puts his hands together as a prayer and replies, "Thank you, Martha. Thanks to your information, I will change my defense strategy."

Martha replies, "You're better off and now squeeze your ass and go in that he is waiting for you."

Cristian walks into Suao's office and sits in front of Suao.

"I think you have something to tell me about your trip to Miami. I'm all ears."

Cristian felt a chill on his back, but he had to face the situation, so he did not think twice, and tells him in great detail whose idea it was, what was the purpose of the interview and how they had spied on Nick's headquarters to do the interview. Cristian also stated that Juan did not know what was happening when he went to Miami. Suao listens to him to the end and asks him.

"Why did you do it, knowing that everything was wrong from the beginning?"

Cristian responds firmly, "I did it because I want the best for the country. Nicholas Field is a time bomb that can explode. We will all suffer the consequences if we give the power of the most powerful country in the world to a person with no experience about anything and with such a controversial personality as Mr. Field. I understand that in the process, it would benefit Governor Charles, but that is the last thing of importance to me."

Suao reclines in his chair and replies, "You are a very talented man, that's why you are our star reporter. Your sword is your lexicon, and you are a master using it. I know you do not lie to me when you tell me about the sequence of events of what happened. Also, I am not the one to say that you lie about the reason you did it, even though I don't believe you. Only you know the truth, but lying to me and using the channel to benefit a candidate politically is unacceptable. That goes against the principles of our channel. Here we give the same opportunity to any candidate who wants to buy airtime or run a paid political ad, whether we agree with the content. If you believe Nicholas Field is insane, objectively present the facts that support your theory and let the viewers make their own conclusions. Your job on this channel is to inform and not to be a political activist. I suspended you from employment and salary for three months. After three months, you can come back if you think you can respect the rules of our channel. Do you have questions?"

Cristian responds immediately. "No, I think you do the right thing from your point of view, and I did the right thing from mine. I accept that the interview was not lawfully conducted, so I also accept the consequences of my actions. Many will immediately notice and question my absence from the channel. Just as the interview was indisputably very positive for the channel, my suspension can have a negative effect. I am not asking you to reconsider, but to keep in mind that decisions made under an impulsive state of mind are often not the right ones."

Suao responds slowly. "Believe me, it's difficult for me to take such a drastic measure, I know I can lose you and that would be a big loss for our channel, but if you decide to come back, I want it to be your own decision and that you accept the established rules that differentiate us from the other channels."

While leaving the channel, Berry meets Juan again in the parking lot. They both look at each other and Juan asks. "How long did they give you?"

"Three months. And how long was yours?"

Juan responds angrily, "One month, but if I came to know your plan, I would never have gone. The Cuban Santeria of Miami protects that Viking son of a bitch. He has all those sorcerers working for him. That's why everyone who tries to fuck him ends up fucked up, and we are not the exception."

"I don't believe in that shit." Cristian responds contemptuously.

"If you don't believe, then keep messing with him." Juan tells him defiantly.

"Just because I don't believe doesn't mean I'm going to take the risk; I will never touch that guy again, even with a ten-foot poll." Cristian replies and the two laugh.

CHAPTER TEN

Meeting with Nelson Leal.

Cristian's suspension was immediately noticed, and the channel stated Cristian was on a special mission, therefor, he would be off the air for three months. The figure of Cristian was too important to disappear for three months without suspicions being raised. There were rumors he was sick, that he had problems with the channel and many other theories.

Republicans knew that the only beneficiary of Nick's surprise interview would be Charles, so they took on figuring out the truth about what had happened. It didn't take long to get someone who, for a little money, divulged in great detail what had happened. The news exploded like a surprise torpedo that sank the Democratic ship.

The only favored was Nick, who was only in first place in the polls and Charles moved to a third place. This was because it was Charles's second scandal. The first with the radio announcer Daniel Vertuchi from which he recovered, but now with Cristian he was deeply wounded.

The Democratic Party has an emergency meeting behind closed doors to discuss the terrible situation created by Charles. The coordinator of the party, Mr. Ronald White, addresses everyone present in the meeting and says.

"Charles has lost all chances of achieving the presidency. Fox reporters took host Cristian by surprise as he left his home and asked him if he and Charles had agreed to ambush Field with the interview, and Cristian only said he had nothing to say about it. That to the public is admitting the facts. The only way to keep the White House is to recruit Nicholas Field into our party. We know the Republicans dealt with this before, but in their arrogance, they thought that Mr. Field would feel honored and would thank them for the offer. "Nicholas practically kicked them out of his headquarters. I propose Nelson Leal to go to Miami and convince Nicholas. Nelson has strong contact with the Latino community in South Florida. He can do some excellent research there to find the best way to negotiate with Mr. Field before meeting him. Does anyone have a better idea or a suggestion?"

No one said a word. Everyone knew that what Ronald said was true and that time was running out.

The student movement of Nick's campaign was getting stronger and stronger. In the universities around the nation, students wore a T-shirts with Nick's face with a Viking helmet and underneath it said, "MY PRESIDENT."

Nelson Leal contacts Democratic commissioner Angel Martinez and asks for his help in collecting personal information about Nick. Martinez felt a chill on his back.

After the bitter experience he had with Nick, he preferred to stay away as much as possible.

"Yes, of course, Nelson. I will gladly help you in any way I can. Unfortunately, I can't do it personally because of my workload, but I will put you in touch with Santiago Benitez who is very talented and trustworthy."

Martinez calls Santiago immediately and says, "Hi Santiago, I have the perfect job for you that will give you the connections you need. On Tuesday, Nelson Leal arrives in Miami; Nelson has an influential position in the party and needs your help."

Santiago excitedly replies, "What does he need?"

"He needs you to collect as much information as possible about the fricking Viking and, above all, to look for dirty laundry. The rest he takes care of."

Santiago's face changes as if he were looking at a ghost.

"Are you crazy? You know well that whoever messes with that guy ends upside down. Do you forget what happened to you? Did you forget he wiped out Commissioner Otero's family? I don't believe in witchcraft but doesn't mean it doesn't exist." Santiago hangs up the phone without saying goodbye.

Martinez throws the phone angrily, "Asshole! Let me see who I can find now."

Martinez pulls out a notebook he of kept from people who owed him favors or who were trying to earn a seat in the party. Suddenly he sees the name of Benito Heredia who was an ambitious young man with few scruples.

"Hello Benito, today is your lucky day. I have the job that will open the doors for you at the party; remember me when you get to the top. I hope you don't forget that it was me who recommended you, even though others said that you would not measure up."

Benito excitedly replies, "You know I am competent and grateful to those who help me. What do I have to do?"

Martinez crosses his fingers and replies.

"You just have to gather as much information as you can about Nicholas Field. If you can get dirty laundry, you win the lottery. On Tuesday, Nelson Leal arrives in Miami, and you will work with him directly. Nelson is one of the top-ranking people in the party, so I need you to be professional and efficient in this, especially not a word to anyone."

Benito proudly replies, "You select the right person. You don't have to worry about it."

Nick's campaign seemed unstoppable. Eric Wilson installed a security system at the Headquarters and at Nick's house that made it impossible for intruders to approach without being detected. It ordered that only two computers at headquarters should have access to the Internet and that those computers could not keep any confidential information to prevent hackers from stealing information. The rest of the computers are used to store information and did not communicate with each other. Steve took checking the sites where Nick was scheduled to attend and only, if he considered it safe, would Nick attend. Stanley became Nick's shadow, only separating from Nick when he left him at home at night.

Nelson is met at the airport by Benito, who poured him out of flattery, trying to earn points with Nelson. Benito was tall, thin, with curly brown-hair. His presence was sloppy and unpleasant, but Nelson had the consolation that his stay in Miami would be temporary.

Benito had a reputation for having contacts in all social spheres and especially in the darkest. Nelson shakes Benito's hand and says, "I have good references for you. What is your plan?"

Benito feels important, smiles and responds. "I have a friend who is a computer expert and I'm sure he will hack Mr. Field's computers."

Nelson stops and looks at Benito. "What your friend is going to do is illegal, so I didn't hear what you said, neither know what you're talking about. Just give me what you find out without telling me how you did it. Find out with neighbors anything, it doesn't have to be negative. I'm interested to know in what he spends his free time, and who his friends are. I only have three days, so you have to move fast."

The next day, before closing the headquarters, Wilson meets with everyone and tells them, "A well know hacker hacked our computers. He couldn't get anything because we have nothing related to the campaign. Then I hacked the hacker's computer and saw that he went into every available site, searching for information about Nick. The IP address belongs to an individual known for engaging in cyber fraud. We don't know if our cell phones are safe, so no one should talk about our operations on the phone after leaving here."

Nick scratches his head and says, "These people don't get tired of fucking with us. What is your plan?"

Wilson, with his characteristic coldness, responds, "I hired a private detective and gave him the address of the hacker. He will take pictures of who he meets, and we will find out who he works for."

The next day, Wilson gives an update on his research.

"We have the information we need. The hacker works for Benito Heredia, who relates to members of the Democratic Party. I don't know if he's a member or just looking for favors."

Nick, surprised, asks. "How do you know that?"

"My private investigator took the picture of Benito Heredia's car when he went to the hacker's house. The license plate of the car is registered to a certain Benito Heredia. Then he searched the social media and the photo of the person getting out of the car matches the person on social media named Benito Heredia."

Namir interrupts, "Is that Benito working for someone else?"

Wilson, with his usual patience, replies, "You're right."

Stanley, seeing that Wilson does not just speak, says enraged, "Talk at once. You are a fucking turtle."

Wilson moves his head slowly and replies.

"I take my time, so I don't make mistakes. I told my investigator to forget about the hacker and to follow Benito. That Benito is working for Nelson Leal. My investigator took pictures of the two of them at a Miami Beach hotel, then with a small bribe to the hotel server, he got the room number where Nelson was staying. With another small bribe, he got the name of the person staying in that room. That's how we got to Nelson, a senior member of the Democratic Party. I later verified all this on the social media. "

Steve shows off his knowledge of counterintelligence and says, "I have a plan. Tonight, I'm going to write an email to Nick from an internet café for the hacker to intercept and then they kill each other."

Everyone laughs.

The next morning, Nelson calls Benito.

"Hello Benito, bring me everything you have today at twelve to my hotel. This afternoon I will go to Nicholas' headquarters I have no appointment, but I will go anyway."

Benito responds like a soldier to his sergeant, "I will be at twelve o'clock in the same place."

At ten in the morning, Benito calls the hacker and says, "I will go at eleven in the morning to your house, gather everything you have, and I will give you your money."

The hacker replies, "I couldn't really get anything you can use against your Viking, but there's one thing your boss should know. It's very compromising."

Benito decides not to waste time and leaves immediately to the hacker's house. Benito pays the hacker five hundred dollars in cash and the hacker only gives him the copy of an email.

Benito reads it and exclaims, "Son of a bitch! Your betrayal will cost you a lot! "

Benito meets Nelson at the hotel and tells him, "We had no luck getting information that could pressure Mr. Field, but it was worth the try and the money. We have discovered a traitor who is working for the enemy."

Benito gives the email to Nelson and Nelson reads:

"Dear Nicholas Field, above all, thank you for the opportunity you have given me to work on your campaign, even if it is anonymously. It is a privilege for me to be on your side, as you have shown that you have the leadership that is so needed in these difficult times. I ask you not to misinterpret my refusal to leave the ranks of the Democratic Party, so that they would not see it as treason or opportunism. I am more useful to you from within the ranks of the party than outside.

I know that many will accuse me and catalog me of every negative thing they can imagine, but that does not matter to me because the future of my country, my state and that of the thousands of residents who put their vote and their trust in me go before that.

I wish you luck and health.

Angel Martinez."

Nelson puts both hands on his forehead and quietly trying to restrain himself exclaims, "That son of a bitch, traitor, is going to cry tears of blood."

Benito takes the opportunity to win more points.

"Now, I understand why Martinez didn't want to meet you at the airport and entrusted this to me. I am sure he has not even called you."

Nelson replies, "Even worse, he calls me every day asking if I've found out anything."

Benito replies, "Of course, so he could tell the Viking. What are you going to do now with that bastard?"

Nelson takes a deep breath. "I'm going to Nicholas' headquarters. That was the goal of my visit and once and for all, I will confirm if Martinez is a rat."

Benito once again seizes the opportunity. "You must do a deep cleaning here. I am sure Martinez is not the only traitor. You can count on me unconditionally for anything. Don't forget my phone number. We have to fight together on this."

Namir greeted Mr. Nelson Leal at the headquarters. "Good afternoon, Mr. Nelson Leal."

When Namir called Nelson by his first and last name, Nelson felt like a boxer who receives a punch and he is still standing; but he sees colored lights and little birds flying and singing around his head.

"Excuse me, young lady. Do we know each other?" Nelson questions.

"You don't know me, but I know you. You're a prominent member of the Democratic Party and you're coming to talk to Mr. Nicholas Field. Aren't you?"

Nelson knew he was not that prominent, so Namir couldn't know him by his first and last name. Someone had passed that information to them. That confirmed that Martinez was a rat.

"You are absolutely right. You are very efficient, I congratulate you. I would like to have a few words with Mr. Field."

Namir smiles and replies, "Mr. Field is waiting for you. He told me you would come today, but I didn't know what time."

Nelson felt he was short of breath. Only Martinez and Benito knew he was going to Nick's headquarters that afternoon. "Thank you, very much young lady; you are very kind."

Nelson enters the small office and is impressed. How have these guys been able to do such a campaign with no budget?

Nick asks him to sit down, and Nelson sits across from Nick. Nelson stares at a folder Nick had on his desk. Nick lies back on his chair, a second-hand chair bought at the flea market which springs squeak, giving the impression that it would break at any moment. Nelson did not know where to start. There were so many doubts and impressions that his mind had been blocked.

Nick sees the despair on Nelson's face. Nelson had swallowed the hook of the email. Nick, seeing that Nelson did not speak, he tells him, "In times of war, it is the duty of the captain of the victorious ship to rescue the sailors from the sunken ship."

Nelson, confused, replies, "I don't understand what you want to tell me."

Nick shrugs his shoulders and replies, "I want to tell you that if you want to join our ranks, you will be welcome.

We have welcomed others before you, and we guarantee discretion."

Nelson swallowed the hook more and more; he was already almost one hundred percent sure that Martinez had betrayed the party. Nelson tries to recover and responds.

"Be careful who you rescue and recruit. Remember that the first to leave the ship are the rats."

Nick points his finger at him and replies, "You're absolutely right, but that's another topic. Now, let's get to the purpose of your visit. What am I good for?"

Nelson takes a deep breath and decides, "We want to propose to you that...."

Nick raises both hands as a stop. "If you come to propose me to join the Democratic Party, here I have the answer."

Nick gives the folder to Nelson. Nelson opens it, and he can't believe his eyes. The first thing he sees is a picture of Benito entering the hacker's house, then a photo of him and Benito at the hotel and then a sheet of paper with a NO! written in red. "As you can see, I also have my informants. You are not only a participant in a crime, but you do not regret committing it. Our interview has been brief, but productive. You taught me something. I shouldn't have offered you to join the crew of my ship. I don't want rats on my ship. Have a good day."

Nelson left the headquarters as fast as he could. His blood pressure was at the point of a heart attack. Nelson calls Benito to reconfirm once again that Commissioner Angel Martinez was a traitorous rat. "Benito is me, Nelson.

I need to know something. It is extremely important that you think before you answer."

Benito, surprised by the call, answers, "Ask and you can be sure that my answer is one hundred percent true."

"Who knew about my stay and the purpose of my visit to Miami?"

Benito responds immediately, "Martinez informed me of your visit and the purpose; I told no one else. The hacker doesn't know who that assignment was for, but I can't tell you if Martinez informed anyone else."

Nelson closes his eyes and takes a deep breath, trying to control his helplessness. "Did Martinez know that Nicholas' computer system would be compromised?"

"No! I never told him anything. That's illegal and the fewer people know about it, the better."

Nelson closed his eyes, put both his hands on the steering wheel of his car, and laid his head on his hands. Benito's answers drove the final nails into Martinez's political coffin. There was no doubt that Martinez was a traitor and had kept Nick informed all along. The high-resolution camera system installed by Wilson had allowed them to follow Nelson to his vehicle. The entire group gathered in the camera monitoring room; it was like they were watching a comedy movie where Nelson was the Oscar-winning actor. Nelson had lost control and hit the steering wheel with his two fists and shouted, "Martinez, son of a bitch, I'm going to make you pay."

The cameras were so powerful that they could capture even Nelson's facial expression. The group laughed out loud, and Nick had to hold on to Brandon and Stanley so as not to lose balance, and then sat on the floor to unleash his emotions. Namir runs out of the room and Victor asks.

"What's wrong with you? Where are you going?"

Namir replies, "I can't take it anymore. I think I've peed."

That night, they partied, and they all went to dinner at a Chinese buffet. It was the first time that they all went out together including Nick's family, since Stanley, as head of security, did not allow it. Nick thanks Stanley for including Steve Donovan and Eric Wilson to the group.

The news that Nick was at the Chinese buffet quickly spread and it filled the buffet with curious and some reporters. A reporter asks Nick.

"Why do you run away from the press and decline to give interviews? What are you afraid of?"

Raul Fernandez, the campaign's spokesperson, and former Hispanic news anchor, responds. "Nicholas Field does not run away from the press. It is the lack of time that prevents him from doing so. Campaigning, supervising a business, and not neglecting the family is an almost impossible mission for a single person."

The reporter mockingly replies, "That very thing you have said, he could have said, but even that, you had to say for him."

Nick takes the reporter's words as a personal insult, stands up and responds. "When and where do you want the interview?"

The surprised reporter replies, "I don't have questions prepared for you, but if you will allow me, I would like to ask them the day after tomorrow."

Nick raises his glass of water and ridiculing the reporter, says, "I ask for a toast for our reporter, who says I run away from the press, but when I give him the opportunity, he runs away from me."

The reporter did not expect Nick's answer. "Don't get me wrong Mr. Field, I don't have questions prepared for you. I would like to ask you questions of interest to everyone and not waste time on silly questions."

"Well, I don't need two days to prepare my answers to your questions. That's why I told you that whenever and wherever you want, I will answer them. Prepare your questions. You can also ask my adversaries for help; they will be more than happy to help you. Remember that there can only be only three questions." Nick replies.

"Why just three questions?"

Nick puts his hand on the reporter's shoulder and says, "Because every day I answer three questions from the emails that I receive, and that space will be for you. Now if you will not ask me questions, I invite you to dinner with us. If you give your word that you won't talk about politics over dinner."

The reporter did not miss the opportunity and sat down with them to enjoy the dinner.

Nelson meets in the headquarters' offices of the Democratic Party with senior party leaders. Everyone was eager to know the results of Nelson's mission. Party chairperson Ronald White tells Nelson, "Give us good news, please. You scare me with that face."

Nelson responds. "The interview did not last even ten minutes. The only thing that the trip accomplished was to discover that Commissioner Martinez is a rat, and that Florida is lost. How can we win a state where our key men work for the enemy? From today on, we must divert campaign funds to other states."

Absolute silence reigned in the office; Ronald's face was one of total bewilderment. Nelson throws the folder that Nick had given him with the photos.

"Commissioner Martinez didn't come to meet me at the airport, citing that he had been exposed to the coronavirus and was overwhelmed with work. Some Benito met me and assisted me throughout the time. Martinez would call me every day to ask me what I had achieved and then pass it on to the fucking Viking. Benito, through a hacker, hacked the Nicholas' computer system. Martinez had no knowledge that Nicholas' system had been hacked and here I have proof of his betrayal via the email he sent to Nicholas."

Nelson passes the copy of the mail to everyone to read and the two photos. "The first photo is of Benito entering the hacker's house. The second photo is of Benito meeting me at the hotel restaurant. Only Martinez and Benito knew of my presence in Miami. When I arrived at the headquarters of the Viking, the secretary called me by my first and last name, then she told me that Nicholas was waiting for me in his office. He told me that if I wanted to join his group, they would welcome me. I would not be the first to do so. He rubbed in the face that Martinez already worked for him."

Party secretary Thomas Johnson shouts, "I'm going to call that son of a bitch right now and he's going to have to listen to me!"

Ronald holds him by the arm and says, "You can't do that, Martinez can give us away. Remember that the hacker worked for us and that makes us an accomplice to a crime. What I don't understand is why Mr. Field didn't report us for hacking his system. "

Nelson responds, "He is an enigma. Our informant told us that the Republicans tried to recruit him and used not very legal methods. However, he did not give them away. My opinion is that he keeps it as a card up his sleeve for the right moment."

Thomas angrily asks, "What are we going to do with Martinez?"

Ronald replies, "For now nothing, he is not in for re-election at the moment, and it would be bad propaganda for the party. We do not need more scandals. Let's look for his replacement right now and when the time comes for re-election, we cut off the light and water to that filthy rat."

CHAPTER ELEVEN

The end of the campaign.

The reporter to whom Nick had granted the interview was an independent reporter who did not think twice about contacting the national networks looking for the highest bidder. On the day agreed for the interview, a reporter from the MCNTV network arrives. Nick asks in surprise, "Where is the reporter who wanted to interview me? Where did you guys come from?"

The reporter replies, "He contacted us and told us he was not qualified for such an interview and gave us the opportunity."

Nick looks at him seriously and replies, "Let's not start disrespecting each other. He sold the interview to you. I have nothing against him about what he did. He saw the opportunity to make good money, and he took it."

The reporter replies, "Those are your conclusions, and I don't plan to waste my time talking about it when we have so many important things to talk about. If you are ready, we could start now."

Nick moves his head affirmatively and says, "I'm all yours whenever you want to."

"Good afternoon, I'm John Walls from MNCTV. broadcasting live from Nicholas Field's headquarters. First, I would like to thank Mr. Field for giving us this opportunity. I know you are a person who the only thing you lack is time, therefore I only have time to ask you three questions. There is concern for the religious community that you will not represent them, for it is known that you have not baptized your children and do not go to any church. Are you an atheist?"

John Walls task was to turn as many voters as possible against Nick and what better question to turn voters against him than one about religion. Nick understands John will attack him with heavy artillery and that he would have to defend himself like a cat on his back.

"Mr. Walls, have you read the Bible?"

"Yes, I've read it. I study at a Catholic school in New York."

"So can you tell me which church the Bible says we should go to?"

The reporter also understood that battle would not be easy since Nick knows how to defend himself and fight back at the same time.

"No, the Bible does not specify any religion or church."

Nick points his finger at him and replies. "Exactly, because God only gave us the Ten Commandments to follow. Believe me, if we were to respect and follow the Ten Commandments, we would not need so many churches and religions. God is everywhere and I advise you that before you seek God in a church, bring him into your heart. That is the perfect place for him. I do not criticize the believer who in good faith goes to church, whatever it may be. I have met religious people of all kinds of religions who I respect because they practice what they preach. I have also met people who use religion as a business and to enrich themselves. Others believe they can sin the entire week and that by attending church on Sunday or donating money to the church are already free from sin. I detest religious hypocrisy. Pope Francis asks for help for refugees, but has never given a penny for them, while charging for Vatican admission, baptisms, and masses. In Bolivia, former President Ebo Morales gave him a gift with the communist symbol of the sickle and hammer. Pope Francis accepted it without protest. He accepted it without caring that the communists have persecuted and eliminated millions of religious people. Which rabbi would have accepted a gift with the Nazi Swastika? I admire the late Pope John Paul II and St. Francis; they were truly religious and like them there are thousands. It is not only a Catholics problem, in all religions there are opportunists and good people. There are many prophets, such as the case of James Jones in George Town Guyana, who, when he felt cornered, poisoned his parishioners with cyanide. Nine hundred and eighteen people died, including two hundred and sixty children.

I only believe in God and let others believe in their God, whatever it may be. All religions preach the same thing, doing good and loving our neighbors. No one should worry that I do not attend a certain church, but they should worry and distrust those who use religion for political purposes. I love freedom, and that includes freedom of religion."

The journalist, seeing that he had not achieved his goal tries another angle. "Based on your comments, it is correct to say that you have no fear of God."

Nick replies, "You're absolutely right. I'm not afraid of God. Why should I fear him? The Bible says that God is love. God should be obeyed and respected, not feared. God is there to help and protect us. A true father does not want his children to fear him; he prefers to be loved and obeyed. Children who fear their parents do not share their problems with them and there is no communication between them. Love generates the basis for a child to trust his parents. I advise you not to fear God; God loves you, protects you, and if you truly repent from your sins, he forgives you.

The reporter, seeing that he did not meet his objectives, changed the subject and searched for a topic where he believed Nick was not updated, "The world is getting smaller and smaller with the advancement of technology. I understand you dislike the idea of globalization and that would be like separating us from the rest of the world and falling behind in all aspects."

"You are wrong again friend, that I am not a supporter of globalization. That does not mean that I am against trading with everyone. Globalization is dependency on others. I think it's the worst mistake a nation can make.

You cannot be totally free if you depend on someone or something. Countries make alliances for convenience and break them when it doesn't suit them. Europe depends on the Russian gas, Russia invades Ukraine and Europe puts sanctions against Russia; Russia cuts off gas supplies to Europe, now Europe is in trouble. We were energetically independent during the Trump administration; the Biden administration made us dependent again and we are all suffering the consequences by paying three times the price we used to pay. The gas high price affects the entire economy negatively. We depend on China in medicine and technology; if tomorrow China invades Taiwan we will be in serious trouble. I believe in cooperation between nations, but that differs from globalization. I want an independent country that can fend for itself in difficult times. We can do so, and it is necessary to prepare for the storm before it hits us."

The reporter sees he is not making progress in his goal and makes a comment so that it does not count as a question. "You imply you do not trust our allies."

Nick responds, "Countries put their interests above treaties and give their vote according to their interests. Russia's threat to the Scandinavian peninsula is a reality. Finland is attempting to join Nato to prevent a similar situation to that of Ukraine, but Turkey is against it. Turkey wants Finland to hand over refugees in Finland who Turkey labels as terrorists. Finland refuses to hand them over, so Turkey punishes Finland with the vote against Finland's entry into NATO. Turkey could prevent the war in Europe from spreading, but it puts the interest of its nation in the face of the potential death of thousands of people."

Walls sees he hasn't been able to put Nick against the ropes and brings out his last question. Walls held the most sensitive and controversial issue in the country for the last. No matter which side Nick takes, this will put a lot of voters against him.

"School killings have become routine, but the government can't reach an agreement because the NRA is a powerful organization that contributes to both Republicans and Democrats and relies on the constitutional right to bear arms. What measures will you take to control firearms?"

"The problem is that we have always been trying to treat the symptoms and not the cause. Guns don't kill anyone; people are the ones who kill through guns. They can buy a tank if they want, that's not the problem. We must hold everyone who related to the weapons accountable. After a multiple murder like the ones that happened in schools, it is very easy to say, "I DIDN'T KNOW ANYTHING." "HE HAD MENTAL PROBLEMS." If we hold directly and indirectly accountable all the people who live in the house where the gun came from to commit the crime, I assure you that there will be over ten eyes supervising each weapon. If one of the family members sees something suspicious, they will notify the authorities immediately and then the responsibility lies with the authorities. That weapon must be seized and kept in a secured place until the person who started the case and the owner of the weapon agree that the weapon can be returned. You must pass a psychological exam to own a weapon. It is normal to be asked for tests to drive a vehicle, so it must be the same to buy a lethal weapon.

Whoever commits a crime using a firearm in a school loses his constitutional right to trial and receives the death penalty automatically. If you have a gun in your home and you think you cannot guarantee its safety, you can turn it over to the police for safekeeping; you can pick up your gun whenever you want without question. Bullets that pierce bulletproof vests must be banned and it will be a crime to possess them. I think deer don't wear bulletproof vests. It is simple, their constitutional right goes hand to hand with their civil liability and to that you must add the vicarious liability, which is the indirect responsibility of the rest of the family. Unfortunately, society responds more to fears of being sued than when is asked to collaborate voluntarily.

Walls sees no progress in his goals, so he adds another provocative comment to see if Nick falls into the trap, "From what I see, you plan to put a system similar to that of the Islamic Taliban."

Nick looks at him seriously, reddens, and doesn't respond immediately. The reporter cannot hide his joy; he believes he has finally achieved his goal.

"Mr. Field, you don't need to answer if you don't want to. It was a comment, it wasn't a question. Only because of the severity of your measures. That is the closest similar system that I know of."

Nick responds by staring into the camera. "We can label a doctor as a criminal or a lifesaver, depending on the intent of his actions."

The reporter is totally confused. The cameraman was a Nick's sympathizer, so he takes advantage and focuses on the reporter's face. The reporter's face was one of total bewilderment.

"What do you mean by that?"

This time, Nick is the one who smiles. "That's your fourth question. We had agreed only three, but of course I'm going to answer it. If a doctor to save a patient's life amputates his hand because of the advanced state of gangrene, he is a lifesaver. If the same doctor enters a house to steal, and the owner surprises him, both fight and the doctor, armed with a machete, cuts off the hand of the owner of the house. That doctor is a criminal. I do not intend to change our society, but I intend to change how we are fighting against that problem. All the measures put in place by Republicans and Democrats have been totally inefficient. We must take drastic measures during crises. If you want to classify me as a Taliban because I want to save the lives of innocent children, then I will be a Taliban. Ask those parents whose children were killed if they agree to drastic measures that can save the lives of children in school. I have never heard of a shooting in the schools of an Islamic country, even though they have an abundance of weapons and bombs in those places. This is because the punishment is immediate and collective. They don't get publicity from the press, which makes other unhinged and attention-hungry people do the same. My proposal does not violate the constitutional rights to bear arms, I agree with that constitutional right. The only right I want to eradicate is the right that some believe they have to murder innocent people. I want a country like our grandparents had, where you could go to school without metal detector or police in the school, you could go to a concert, a Fourth of July parade and all kinds of congregation events without the fear of being murdered. If to achieve this, I have to take off my Viking helmet to put on the Taliban turban. I do it right now happily. Thank you very much and may God bless you all."

Nick's interview did not produce the results expected by the reporter, increasing even more his popularity. Citizens, angry at both parties for not having any results in mass killings, analyzed Nick's proposal as an alternative that could work without the fear of having to lie down their weapons. Because of the interview, Nick gained two more points. Walter and Charles remained virtually tied in second, but increasingly far from Nick.

The next day at the headquarters during a meeting, Brandon asks Nick a question that took him totally by surprise.

"Nick, is time you think about a vice president. Do you have anyone in mind?"

Nick always had an answer for everything, but this time, he did not know what to answer. Nick never thought that this moment would come. On his face, you could see total bewilderment. When Brandon noticed Nick had no response, he glanced at the rest of the group, who were equally astonished. Nick opens his eyes and raises his eyebrows and says, "Wow! No, a fucking idea."

Everyone laughs irresponsibly. They had improvised everything so much that what began as a party for the students and, out of anger for Nick, turned into an unprecedented achievement. Now reality was knocking on their doors, and they understood that the game was over and that the weight of the responsibility they had to face was enormous.

Both the Republican and Democratic parties had invested large amounts of capital in their candidates, to no avail. Neither the money nor Nick's many enemies had destroyed him. Only a fortunate miracle could give the victory to Walter or Charles, because despite being both tied for second place, they were about twelve points behind Nick in all the official polls.

In a small motel in the city of Miami, two men are dressed in suits, hats and glasses; both try to cover up their true identity. The only thing that set them apart was that one wore a gray suit and the other a black suit. They are sitting at the small table in the motel room with the TV volume all the way up and the wall air conditioning at full throttle. The noise inside the room is such that sitting face to face, they have a hard time listening to each other, but that was the goal to prevent anyone else from being able to hear them. The man dressed in black asks, "What's your name?"

"The one that you want to give me. And yours?"

The man dressed in black smiles, as he doesn't expect that answer. He puts a briefcase on the table and some keys with a cell phone. "I like your answer. You can also call me whatever you want to call me. Here you have half the money and the keys to the apartment. You will enter the apartment on Wednesday morning and will not leave the apartment until Friday when you finish the job. You have everything you need in the apartment so that you do not go out for those three days. If you have an emergency, you use the phone I gave you. As soon as you finish your job, you will go out the emergency stairs where the extraction group will wait for you Do you have questions? "

The man does not respond, just moves his head from side to side takes the briefcase and keys and leaves without saying goodbye. The students were scheduled to hold an activity in front of Pembroke Pines City Hall in neighboring County North of Miami. Representatives of all the different universities in the country would attend this event. This event was of vital importance to Nick's campaign. This would be the final blow to reaffirm himself as the future president of the United States. All the students who wanted to take part could join the event. They only must present their student ID. Victor had organized the event, Brando had approved it, but they had never informed Steve.

Steve walks into Nick's office and asks, "Is it true that you're going to have an event in front of Pembroke Pines City Hall?"

Nick looks at him in surprise and replies, "Yes, on Saturday at three o'clock in the afternoon."

"That can't be. Cancel it. I cannot guarantee your safety."

Nick closes his eyes in disagreement and asks for an emergency meeting with his immediate team. When everyone is gathered, Steve addresses the group. "We agreed you would inform me of every event forty-eight hours in advance so that I could determine if the venue was safe; if I determined it was not safe, I would look for ways to resolve those shortcomings. Today, I learned we will hold an event in front of Pembroke Pines City Hall on Saturday."

Brandon responds in confusion, "Today is Wednesday. There are well over forty-eight hours left. I don't see the big problem."

Victor intervenes. "The space inside the town hall is not enough for the number of people who confirmed their attendance, so we decided to use the front of the town hall. It is a very large plaza where the city had held various events, such as music festivals, Christmas parties, etc. The participants are young, who prefer the outdoors and sitting on the floor. The more informal, the more attractive to them."

Steve looks at Stanley and asks, "You were aware of this and didn't inform me of anything?"

Stanley, confused, replies, "I know you check the venue before the event. I also know that the city of Pembroke Pines will provide ten officers for the event, three traffic patrols, five uniformed officers, and two undercovers. I think it is more than enough."

Steve responds disappointedly. "I can't believe what you say."

Steve looks at Erick, who quickly becomes defensive. "Don't look at me. That's not my specialty."

Nick looks at Stanley and opens his hand like the one asking what's going on. Steve takes a deep breath. He understands it is not their expertise. "I will explain why the event cannot be held:

First, no matter how much security you put in, it's an open field event.

Second, the plaza has a lake that separates the plaza from an apartment's complex located less than five hundred feet away.

Third, all apartments have an uninterrupted view of the plaza.

Fourth, if something happens, the lake prevents us from crossing and leaves us only one way to get to the complex. That road can be easily blocked, and it would take us at least two minutes to get to the complex. By that time, the killer would be away from the scene."

Nick, surprised, asks, "Are you saying that they are preparing a hit on me? Where did you get that information from? I think you're exaggerating."

Steve replies, "I'm not exaggerating. I'm just doing my job. You must cancel the event."

Brandon responds angrily, "Many students are already in Miami. The delegation from Hawaii and Texas arrived yesterday and this morning those from California, Montana, Arkansas and Virginia arrived; five more delegations will arrive this afternoon. This would represent an act of cowardice and that is all our adversaries need to attack us. We cannot give the image of a coward president."

Steve raises his tone of voice, visibly angry. "Don't confuse prudence with cowardice. They are two very different things."

Brando also responds angrily, "They may be different, but they will have the same effect before public opinion."

Nick sees things are getting out of control, so he asks everyone to calm down. "I understand both sides, and they both have their reasons. We need solutions and not arguments. What do you propose?"

Steve responds a little calmer, "The only way we could be a little safer would be to have three snipers on the roof of the town hall guarding the buildings, having two drones flying in front of the buildings during the event to detect any suspicious activity , a police patrol in front of the buildings to stop anyone who wants to escape and finally a helicopter permanently flying the area. But because it is an event in an open space, my recommendation is to cancel the event."

Nick replies, "I take responsibility and try to get what Steve asks for. I will not cancel the event; many students are already in Miami and have come from far away."

Steve shakes his head disenchanted. "I'll try to get everything we need, but I keep saying this is a big mistake."

The night before the event on the third floor of the building facing the plaza, the subject who was hiding receives a phone call.

"Hello, listen and follow the instructions. In the cabinet below the kitchen sink there is a box with two painted canvases reflecting an empty balcony. One is for you to place on the balcony railings and cover the top of it; the other to place it around the railings and reflect the sides of the balcony. So, you can do your job without being detected from any flanks snipers or surveillance drones. In the agreed place, two people will wait for you. They will give you your money and you will leave the complex on a low-speed electric motorcycle which will have a pizza delivery box on the back, no one will suspect that someone who is fleeing will do so at a maximum speed of thirty miles per hour. The pizza box has a false bottom; you will put the briefcase in it and you will leave following the vehicle that gave you the motorcycle at low speed. You will not talk to them and if you speak to them, they will not answer you. If you have questions, ask me now."

The subject did not ask any question, just hung up the phone and went to find the canvases. In the box he found the canvases, a T-shirt and a cap with the logo of a pizzeria. When he took the canvases to the balcony, he saw everything was meticulously planned, since the railings had brooches to secure the canvases, which matched perfectly with the brooches of the canvases. It was night; therefore, no one saw when the subject covered the balcony. It was impossible to detect anyone on the balcony floor, because from all angles, the view of an empty balcony was reflected.

Steve got everything requested, even though it was difficult and cost almost everything they had in the campaign account. Among the guests, students, those who joined them, those who came out of pure curiosity and journalists totaled more than a thousand people in the plaza. Brandon opened the ceremony with a few words that moved everyone.

"Thank you for honoring us with your presence. This is a time for changes, and you have made it possible. I want to start by saying that when there are people who kneel when they hear the national anthem and say they are discriminated against. We stand with our hands on our hearts and feel proud and blessed. Let us stand up to sing our national anthem."

The audience applauded loudly and sang the national anthem. It was the first time that a political act began by singing the national anthem, breaking once again with the traditional. Brandon then gave the floor to the representative from Hawaii, who spoke for about ten minutes. At the command center, Steve Donovan monitors the images transmitted live by the two drones that surveillance the area of the buildings and their surroundings. The drones had focused their cameras on more than one occasion on the subject's balcony, but because it was a distance of more than a hundred feet, the camouflage of the balcony could not be detected.

The subject had his high-caliber sniper rifle on his tripod. It was an easy shot for the experienced sniper, because the weather was perfect, and the distance was less than five hundred feet. He was accustomed to distances of over eight hundred feet, so this work was a gift to him. He had his rifle ready and just waited for Nick to come out to the podium. Steve became more and more nervous; he had a hunch that such a calm was the meaning of a misfortune. Stanley and Nick were with Steve at the command post.

Stanley says, "You have to calm down a little. You're out of control. I've never seen you like this before. What do you want? Do you want to see a man with a rifle?"

Steve responds seriously, "That's what worries me the most; I don't see anyone with a rifle."

Nick takes Stanley by his arm and pulls him aside. "This man is out of control. Stay with him here and monitor him. I am afraid that he will see a ghost and give order to shut. This will become a real tragedy."

Stanley squeezes his lips and raises his eyebrows. He knows Nick is right. " I'll stay with him. I promise you I will control him."

Brandon introduced Nick. The audience goes crazy shouting "THE VIKING, THE VIKING." Nick goes out with his wife and two children to greet the audience. The sniper has him in the crosshair but decides not to shoot and kill him when he is next to his wife and children; he prefers to shoot him when he is alone on the podium.

In the command center, Steve looked at the screens of the security monitors constantly while Stanley monitored the radio transmissions. Steve yelled, "I found you son of a bitch!"

Stanley runs to the monitor and asks, "Where is it?"

"Look Stanley, this building has an uninterrupted view of the plaza. In all the other balconies there are people looking over here with binoculars, except in this apartment on the third floor."

Stanley replies, "Listen to your words. You just said there's no one on the balcony."

Steve, enraged, yells, "Fuck! Get Nick off the podium right now."

Stanley replies, "Calm down please. We have a patrol car in front of that building. I'll contact him and tell him to go up to the third floor and knock on the door of the second apartment from right to left."

Steve stands up from his chair and says, "You take him out or I take him out myself."

Stanley does not answer him, he takes his radio and calls the patrol in front of the building, "Central Command to Unit Six."

The officer replies, "Unit six to central command."

Before Stanley can say anything else, Steve walks toward the exit of the central command post. Stanley knows that if he doesn't stop him, Steve will forcibly drag Nick away from the podium, causing chaos. Both men engage in a struggle and fall to the ground. Namir rushes out to seek help to stop the fight.

Namir enters the central command with an officer, and they see Stanley trying to stop Steve by holding Steve's right leg with his two hands.

"What the fuck is going on here?" The officer shouts.

"Please stop it." Shout Stanley without letting go of Steve's leg.

The screams of horror from the crowd paralyzed everyone. Steve and Stanley ran to the monitors and saw that Nick had been shot, and the crowd was running in different directions. Steve cries inconsolably and bangs on the table. "I knew, I knew it. You didn't listen to me."

Stanley picks up the radio and screams in a hurry. "Central command to unit six, the subject is on the third-floor, second apartment from right to left. Do you copy me?"

The officer replies, "QSL. Copied and on the way."

They wasted precious time while Stanley was trying to stop Steve, that allowed the subject to exit the apartment before the officer arrived.

The subject arrives in record time to the back of the building where two men were waiting for him. He takes the briefcase and puts it inside the false bottom of the distributing the pizzas box, and leaves on the motorcycle after the vehicle that was waiting for him.

Chaos reigned in the plaza; everything had been broadcasted live nationwide. The getaway plan worked. The police were running in a hurry to get to the building and ignored the subject, who was slowly getting away from the scene on a small motorcycle. Suddenly the vehicle in front of the subject speeds up, and the passenger squeezes a detonator with his finger and blows the subject and the motorcycle into the air.

The police break the door of the apartment and find the apartment empty and on the balcony; the rifle mounted on the tripod.

Brittany cried heartbroken over her husband's body that was paling more and more.

"For what? Why all this? If in the end everything has been in vain."

Nick, pulling out his last strength, takes his wife's hand with his two hands and responds.

"Life is lived in vain when you do not fight in the face of injustices. You live in vain when you live in fear. Only you will determine if you want to live in vain or that my effort has been in vain. My journey ends where yours begins. I will be with you forever and ever. Thank you for giving me so much joy during these years and for two beautiful children."

Nick looks at Brandon and says, "This is not the end. This has just begun."

Nick gives one last squeeze to his wife's hands and closes his eyes.

Brittany hugs her dying husband and her white blouse tinted red with her husband's blood.

"I promise you, love, that I will not allow your life and your sacrifice to be in vain."

END.

Printed in the USA
CPSIA information can be obtained
at www.ICGtesting.com
JSHW021936301223
54587JS00001B/28

9 781960 629470